JESSICA WATKINS PRESENTS

KEECE AND *Paris* 2

A MIL-TOWN LOVE STORY

CHARAE LEWIS

Acknowledgments

God we are on another book and I am so grateful. I ran from my gift for years and I am so glad that you've brought me back to doing what I love to do. Thank you for being so faithful to me when I fail you daily. Please continue to guide me to be not only a better writer but a better woman. I love you.

Keon I love the way that you love me. Thank you for being patient with me when I'm forced to get these words out of my head. You are truly the best and I can't ask for a better man to share my life with.

Candace, I love you. You are always there for me when I need you and I appreciate that. I can't wait to see what God has in store for you. Thank you for inspiring my Paris character. You are so strong willed and determined to accomplish you goals. You are truly an inspiration.

Mom and Granny, thank you for making me into the woman that I am today. I love you guys immensely.

To my Lewis, Randolph and Glover squad, I couldn't ask to be born into a better family. I can count on all of you if I needed something and that speak volumes to me. I love you all.

Jessica I appreciate you once again for helping to make my dream a reality. You have challenged me in so many ways to become a better writer and I appreciate that. Thank you for your hard work and for always being there when I need you.

To my JWP family thank you for your continued support. I couldn't ask for a better team to be a part of. Let's keep slaying these charts and writing these amazing books.

To the readers, I am so thankful that you have taken time out of your lives to read my work. I work so hard to bring these characters to life and I'm so happy that you love them just as much as I do. You guys keep me going for real and I pray that I've met your expectations with this second installment.

KEECE AND *Paris* 2
A MIL-TOWN LOVE STORY

CHAPTER ONE

Keece took the phone away from his ear so he could collect his emotions. A lump began to form in his throat as his mouth became dry. He was hoping that what his brother, Case, had just told him was a joke. He was hoping that he would awake from a nightmare, Paris would be right next to him, and his father would be a phone call away.

"What are you saying, Case? Pops killed himself?" Keece asked as his voice cracked.

"I think he tried—"

"What the fuck? Either he's dead or he's alive! Which is it?" Keece yelled, cutting him off.

"Look, nigga, my mom called and said that she wasn't sure if he tried to kill himself, but they're not sure if he is going to make it. She said meet her at St. Mary's."

"A'ight. I'm on my way." Keece hung up.

Keece frantically jumped in the car and started the engine. Initially, he was on a mission to find his lady, Paris, but she had been pushed to the back burner for his father. The fact that Keece had been purposely ignoring his father ate him up inside. If his father didn't survive, Keece knew he would never forgive himself.

After doing ninety on the highway, Keece arrived at the hospital. He found a parking space and then hurried into the emergency room. Keece ran up to the desk to get information about his father, but he was interrupted by Case.

"We don't know anything yet. They told us to wait for the doctor to come out," Case told him with his hand on Keece's shoulder.

Keece then followed Case to the waiting room, where the rest of his brothers were, seated along with his stepmother, Celine. She was wiping her eyes with a tissue while sobbing softly. Keece took a look at Dinero, Kiyan, and Big. He could tell by the looks on their faces that they were fucked up by the news. Despite the drama that had surfaced, Dom had always been a good father to them, and just the thought of losing him caused a sharp pain to shoot through Keece's chest. He sat down next to Kiyan.

"So do y'all know what happened exactly?" Keece asked no one in particular.

Celine slowly removed the tissue from her eyes, and then wiped her nose. Her eyes were red and puffy while a distraught look plastered her face.

"I don't know the whole story, but Fred called and said he had found him unconscious with a bottle of liquor, along with an empty pill bottle," she said softly.

Celine was still on edge whenever she was around the boys, since she was the main reason their biological mother, Rochelle, had been absent from their lives. Celine had lied on Rochelle, telling Dom that she had been sleeping with his right-hand man in order for her to have him to herself. Her plan had worked in her favor for years, until Rochelle showed up and spilled the truth.

Minutes later, Riley came rushing toward Celine. "Hey, I came as soon as I heard the voicemail," she said sitting next to her.

Seeing his ex-girlfriend, Riley, reminded Keece that he was in a fucked up situation with his baby, Paris. He wished he had the time to chase after her to profess his love and ask for her forgiveness, but he had to ensure that his father was okay.

Keece shook his head and then sat back in his chair. Ever since he awoke, his day had been fucked up. He had lost his lady and possibly his father all in one hour. Keece was trying to remain positive and strong, but he would be lying if he said it was easy.

After consoling Celine for almost an hour, Riley walked over and sat next to Keece. He gave her a look that she couldn't quite read and then he quickly turned his head. She wasn't sure why he was dissing her when just last night they were getting along great. Although their conversation hadn't gone in the direction that she'd hoped, Riley still felt like there was no bad blood between them.

"Are you okay?" Riley whispered so the others wouldn't hear her.

Keece simply shook his head and then looked forward. He wasn't in the mood to converse with Riley.

After sitting in silence for almost an hour, the doctor finally came out. Everyone stood and met him halfway, anticipating what he would say.

"Are you the family of Dominic DeMao?" the doctor asked.

"Yes," they all answered in unison.

The doctor sighed. "Well, he's in stable condition as of now. We had to pump his stomach. I must say if he hadn't got to the hospital in time, he would be dead."

"Thank God!" Celine exhaled a sigh of relief. "Can we go see him now?"

"Sure. He's in room number 19."

The doctor walked the family through a pair of double doors that led to the room where Dom was. He also informed them that Dom was very drowsy. When Keece walked in the room, he almost broke down at the sight of his father, who was lying in a hospital bed with multiple intravenous tubes pumping various fluids into his body. Keece had never seen his father in such a state. He walked up to the side of Dom's bed and rubbed his face.

"Damn, Pops, what were you thinking?" Keece asked with tears in his eyes.

Everyone else in the room was trying to hold back tears but found it difficult. Dom was always a dominating presence in each one of their lives, and to see him lying in a hospital bed tore them apart.

Instead of responding, Dom just stared off into space. It was wrong how he'd chosen to deal with Rochelle, the mother of his children, and he knew that his actions of forcing her out of his sons' lives were unforgivable. He was going crazy not being able to speak with his boys. So he concocted this "suicide" plan to reel them in so they could feel sorry for him. Dom knew it was a fucked up plan, but he was willing to do anything just to get in good graces with them. He felt bad for manipulating them, but he'd had no other choice. He wanted the bond that he used to have with them, and he couldn't fathom living his life without a relationship with his boys.

"I'm just going through right now," Dom said solemnly, laying it on thick.

Celine walked over closer to Dom and kissed his cheek. "Baby, we'll get through this, okay?" she said with tears in her eyes.

Dinero and Kiyan shared a look of disdain when Celine spoke those words. She was still on their shit list for the role she'd played in forcing their mother away.

"Despite what we're going through, you know we'll always be here for you," Keece told Dom. "You shouldn't have tried to take yourself out like this. You're better than that."

Dom looked away and let a tear escape his eye. He knew what Keece had said was true, but he was desperate. So he was willing to take the embarrassment as long as his boys remained in his life.

"Why don't we let him get some rest, and you guys can come back later?" Celine suggested.

Everyone agreed and then walked out of the hospital room.

Big jogged up to Keece who was walking at a fast pace. "You okay, bro? You don't look too good."

Keece stopped and faced him. "Man, shit is all fucked up right now. Paris left me this morning before Case called me. I'll explain that shit later, but I'm about to try and go find her. I'll holla at you later."

"A'ight, bro. Hit me," he said, patting Keece's shoulder.

On the way out, Riley called Keece's name and ran up to him. Keece exhaled before she approached him. He didn't want to be bothered with Riley since he was on a mission to find Paris.

"I just wanna let you know that if you need me, I'm here," she said softly and touched his arm.

"Thanks, Riley. I'll keep that in mind." Then, he simply walked out.

CHAPTER TWO

Paris sat listening to Tink's "Route 42 to San Fran" and looking aimlessly out of her bedroom window. The pain she was experiencing was unlike any other pain she'd ever encountered. Paris had never thought that Keece would have the balls to stay out all night. And she never thought it would be with *Riley* of all people. There was no way that she believed that Keece had actually slept in his car after reading the text from Riley. Paris knew deep down that he had been with Riley. For the entire duration of their relationship, the thought of Keece cheating on her had never crossed her mind. He had always assured her that she was the only woman for him. But now, as she looked at her tear-stained face in the reflection in the window, she wasn't so sure.

Paris had managed to keep her condo after she'd moved in with Keece. This was a secret she had kept from him because she didn't want to hear his mouth. She had figured that if things didn't work out with Keece, then she wouldn't have to move back in with her mother.

Camara had been calling Paris, along with Keece, but she wasn't in the mood to speak with anyone at the moment. All she wanted to do was cry herself to sleep. While Paris began to take off her clothes, she heard her doorbell ring.

Who can that be? No one knows that I'm here, except for my mom, she said to herself.

Paris put her shirt back on before she walked to her front door. She looked out of the peephole and saw that it was Keece.

Fuck! My mama runs her fucking mouth too much!

Paris snatched the door open and plastered a wicked look on her face.

"What?" she spat.

Keece barged his way into her condo, slightly pushing her to the side.

"What the fuck you doin' here? I thought you gave this place up," he barked.

Then he started walking through the condo to ensure that Paris didn't have another man there.

Paris began to follow him as he ran through her house like a maniac. "Get your ass out of my house!" she yelled.

Keece stopped walking, and then got in her face. "If you got another nigga in here, I'm liable to beat your ass," he threatened her.

Paris rolled her eyes, and then smacked her lips. "Fuck you! I'm not a cheater like *you*."

"So your sneaky ass kept this place? What was this? Your hideaway where you bring other niggas?" he yelled in her face.

Paris pushed Keece out her face and began to rain punches all over his body. Flashbacks of him lying to her caused her body to be filled with rage.

"How dare you come up in here questioning me when you just spent the night with your ex? Fuck you!" Paris screamed, still swinging her arms wildly.

"Man, calm the fuck down! I didn't spend the night with that bitch!" Keece said, restraining her.

The couple both fought their way over to the couch where Keece managed to pin her arms above her head while lying on top of her. Paris couldn't stop the tears even if she wanted to. She had given every part of her being to this man just for him to only break her heart. She desperately wanted to forgive Keece, but she couldn't fathom the thought of staying with another cheater. She also felt like, if she forgave him for this one mistake, he'd take her kindness for weakness and begin to hurt her more.

"Listen. I didn't come here to fight with you. I need you to listen to me explain what happened."

"Keece, I ain't trying to hear shit you talking about! It's over between us!" she yelled, trying to squirm out of his strong embrace.

"Damn, Paris, at least let me explain myself. I got drunk and passed out in my car. I promise I didn't spend the night with that girl."

Paris smacked her lips. "Well, what the fuck were you doing at her house? Do you think that shit was appropriate?"

"Nah, it wasn't. That's why I'm trying—" Keece pleaded trying to explain, but Paris cut him off.

"Fuck that! Tell it to somebody who gives a fuck! Now get the fuck off of me!" Paris tried to free her arms from his grasp, but failed.

"So you really not gon' hear me out?"

"Right now your words don't mean shit to me, so hell no!"

"A'ight. If you can say that you don't love me anymore and don't want nothing else to do with me, then I'll leave you alone... *forever*. Can you honestly say that?" Keece asked and prayed silently.

Paris looked into his eyes and said the words that he never wanted to hear, but they were the furthest from her truth. "I don't love you enough to be with you. I don't want nothing to do with you anymore."

Keece could literally feel his heart break after those words escaped Paris' lips. A part of him didn't believe her, but then there was another part of him that gave up. If Paris didn't want to hear his side of the story, then he wouldn't beg her to. Without saying another word, Keece reluctantly got up and walked out of the door. Although it would hurt him, he knew that he would have to let Paris go. She'd forced him to make that choice.

Paris, on the other hand, couldn't believe she'd told Keece that she was done, so she hopped up and ran to the door to catch him. As soon as she opened the door, she realized that he had already driven off and turned the corner.

Fuck! What did I just do? she cursed herself.

Paris' mother had always told her that her stubbornness would get her into trouble, and now here she was crying because she had lost the love of her life.

***

"How's that, baby? Are you more comfortable?" Celine asked, propping up Dom's pillow.

Instead of responding, Dom looked at the TV. He was still stuck in the hospital from his fake suicide attempt, and what bothered him the most was that Celine was all in his face, acting like everything had been cool between them. He was still pissed off because of her lies that had ultimately destroyed his family. He could tell that she was walking on pins and needles around him, hoping that he wouldn't bring up the situation.

"Why are you here?" Dom asked her calmly.

Celine turned to look at him with a puzzled look on her face.

"What do you mean? Don't you expect me to be here for you, Dom?" she asked with a fake chuckle.

"No, I don't. *And* I don't appreciate how you're here pretending that everything between us isn't fucked up," he spat.

Celine sighed slowly and collected her thoughts. She knew Dom was still pissed at her, and she couldn't fault him for that. All she wanted to do was be there for her husband without his nasty attitude.

"Listen, baby, I know things between us are rocky, but we'll get through this like we've done many times before."

"No, we won't. You fucked up my family, and now my sons don't even want to fuck with me. I don't have shit to say to you."

Celine sat in the chair next to his bed and threw her hands over her face. To say that she was stressed would be an understatement. "Dom, I said I was sorry—"

"Sorry ain't enough! I trusted your word and believed that my woman was fucking my best friend. *You* allowed me to keep her away from my boys, although she hadn't done shit wrong! Do you know how I feel? It doesn't make me feel like a man, Celine! Now my sons don't have any respect for me!" Dom yelled, adjusting his body in the bed.

"I understand, Dom, but—"

"You don't understand shit! What the fuck don't you get? You can't fix this shit! Our relationship will never be the same! This is your fuck up, and I was dumb enough to go along with it. I should've never fucked with you!" Dom spat with spittle coming out of his mouth.

Celine stood up, appalled at Dom's revelation. He had never spoken this ill about her, and it caused her heart to break. He couldn't possibly believe that their union was a mistake when she had been the best wife to him and a good stepmother to his sons.

When Celine first laid eyes on Dom, it was the summer of '85. She declared at that moment that she had to have him. The only problem was he was interested in *Rochelle*. Celine tried not to be jealous of Rochelle, but it was hard when Dom took Rochelle out of her aunt's home and upgraded her lifestyle drastically. It also didn't help that Rochelle would brag to Celine about what Dom had purchased for her and all the wonderful things he did for her. So for years, Celine sat back and played the best friend role, until enough was enough. She had her first plan prepared, until Rochelle popped up pregnant with Kiyan. Soon afterward, Keece and Dinero came along.

After Dinero was born, Celine put another plan together that she knew Dom would fall for. Since Rochelle and Dom's right-hand man, Carlos, had grown up together, she figured planting a seed about them fucking around would be a perfect story for Dom to believe. When she told him about it, he lost it. Dom kicked Rochelle out, making sure she didn't take his sons with her. Celine was so happy that he had finally gotten rid of Rochelle that she couldn't contain herself. Rochelle had tried calling Celine numerous times for help, but Celine would ignore her calls and had refused to answer her door.

Soon after Rochelle's departure, Celine came onto Dom, and he took the bait. She ended up playing the good girlfriend and stepmother role so well that he put a ring on it. Celine was in marital bliss and was pleased with her handiwork. Now she loved the boys with all of her heart and truly looked at them as her own. However, the older she got, the more the guilt plagued her conscience. She had never intended for them to find out the truth, but when Rochelle showed up at her house that day, she had no choice but to admit the truth.

Now, she was alone, forced to deal with the repercussions of her actions.

Celine stood up and walked frantically over to the bed. She leaned into Dom's face as she spoke. "Dom, you don't mean that. Please don't say that."

"I do mean it! I can't stand to be in the same room as your scandalous ass. I want a divorce," Dom declared, not even bothering to look at her.

Celine felt like all of the blood in her body had rushed to her feet as her hands became sweaty. Dom had just demanded a divorce, and that fact alone made her almost faint.

"A *divorce?*" she asked visibly hurt.

KEECE AND PARIS 2

"Yes, I'm done with this marriage. It was either stay in the marriage and lose my sons forever, or divorce you and attempt to mend my relationship with them. I'll rather live being a father than a husband to *you* any day."

"Dom, what about *Case*? Don't you think he deserves both of his parents together?" she pleaded, trying to hold Dom's hand, but he snatched away.

"Celine, you're not thinking about Case. Your ass is thinking about *yourself,* as usual. Besides, Case is twenty years old. I'm sure he'll understand."

"Dom, please don't do this. We can get through this. I love you," Celine cried, dropping to her knees.

"Celine, you look *pathetic*. Get up and have some dignity about yourself. You did this, not me. I'll have the lawyer contact you tomorrow." Then Dom pressed the button for his nurse and waited.

Moments later, his nurse walked in.

"What do you need, Mr. DeMao?" the nurse asked.

"Can you please escort her out of my room?" Dom said, pointing to Celine.

"Dom, don't do this," Celine cried, visibly pained by his cold demeanor.

"Ma'am, I'm going to have to ask you to leave," the nurse said.

17

Celine shook her head as tears painted her face. She couldn't believe Dom had just kicked her out of his room. She wanted to protest, but she didn't want to cause a scene. She grabbed her purse and gave Dom one more look before she walked out.

Celine felt like she had been stabbed in the heart. She never thought Dom would leave her. She thought they would make it through any situation thrown their way. Celine now knew that she could never have had a happy ending because she had ruined the lives of too many people. She knew that karma would come back to bite her in the ass, but she didn't expect the pain to be so great.

CHAPTER THREE

Keece sat back looking into the faces of his brothers as he awaited their response. They were at Big's house seated in the living room. He had just filled them in on what had happened between him and Paris. After leaving Paris' condo, Keece had felt worse than he had before. He couldn't believe Paris had actually looked him in his eyes and told him that she didn't love him anymore. Deep down he knew it wasn't true, but he was unwilling to stay and beg Paris. Keece took pride in being a real man, and, even though he loved Paris to his core, he would *never* beg her to stay with him.

"Damn, so Paris just flat out told you she was done fucking with you?" Big asked, taking a sip from his beer.

Keece shook his head, and then threw back his shot of Hennessey.

"Damn, bro, you really got caught up for real. You were supposed to have a lock on your phone," Kiyan joked.

"You think Riley sent that text on purpose?" Case asked.

"I don't know. There ain't no telling. If I had known all this shit was gon' happen, I would've kept my ass at home," Keece said chuckling.

"Aye, why you keep dealing with Riley, though?" Dinero agitatedly spoke. "I mean, come on. You really didn't need that shit she was tryin' to give you. It's obvious that she ain't no good for you 'cause look at how you lost Paris. Even when y'all were together all of those years, what did you have to show for it? She's just an ain't-shit-bitch."

"*Damn*! Nigga, why *you* so mad?" Kiyan inquired.

"Cause I hate that bitch, and the way she did Keece while he was locked up was foul. If I were you, that bitch would be blocked out of my life," Dinero responded.

Keece knew what Dinero had just said was right. Nothing good had come from being associated with Riley. Even though he knew she had a good heart, Keece realized it was time to really go their separate ways. Riley had cost him his relationship with Paris, but he knew that she wasn't totally at fault. He should've never put himself in the position to look as though he may have cheated.

Keece was tired of talking about his depressing love life, so he switched the topic. "Aye, what the fuck was Pops on when he tried to kill himself and shit?"

"On the real, I'm glad he survived, but I can't respect a man who tried to take himself out," Kiyan admitted.

"I don't even know what to say about that shit. That ain't even his character to really try to kill himself. It's basically like he said fuck us," Dinero added.

Big shook his head. "Y'all know I love Dom as if he were my real father, but that was some sucka shit."

Keece noticed that Case was sitting quietly with tears in his eyes. Abruptly, Case got up and walked out of the room. Everyone shared a look. Then Keece got up to go see about him. He found him sitting in the kitchen going through his phone.

Keece took a seat next to him. "Bro, you good?"

Case released a sigh before speaking. "Yeah. I'm just fucked up about everything. Pops told my mom that he wants a divorce. She called me crying and shit, and honestly, I didn't know how to comfort her. I know you don't fuck with my mama, but she's still my mother, and I don't like to see her in any pain."

Keece took in what Case had just revealed to him. Keece hadn't considered Case's feelings about everything, and he honestly felt bad. He hated for his baby brother to be stuck in this messy situation, but it was out of his control.

"Look, I don't know what to say regarding your mom and Pops' situation, but you know that all of us are here for

21

you, regardless of the circumstances. Trust me, we'll all get through this. It'll just take some time." Then Keece gave him a brotherly hug.

"I appreciate that, bro."

"Now come get your ass spanked in Madden."

CHAPTER FOUR

6 months later...

"Okay, now push! 10...9...8..."

Camara had been in labor for ten hours now, and she had been pushing for what felt like forever.. Going through a natural birth proved to be a painful experience for her. Kiyan stood on the right side of her, holding her leg up. Camara's mother, Denise, stood on the other side of her, awaiting her first grandchild's arrival.

"I'm too tired. I can't do it," Camara huffed, shaking her head.

"I know you're tired, but we have to get the baby out. It's been hours since you've started pushing and you've made no progress. Do you want us to use the ventouse?" the doctor asked.

"No, no. I'll try again."

Camara braced herself and pushed like her life depended on it. After a couple seconds, she heard the cries of her baby girl.

As the doctor lay the baby on Camara's stomach, he announced, "She's a beauty."

Camara looked at her daughter in awe, as she screamed at the tops of her lungs. She had thick black curly hair and eyes like her father. She couldn't believe that she was now someone's mother, but, nonetheless, she was happy.

Her pregnancy hadn't been an easy one, but she considered it well worth it. After reaching five months, Camara had cut Kiyan off completely. The cheating, lying and mood swings had become unbearable for her. She was tired of begging Kiyan to be the man that she needed and her heart couldn't take the different women that Kiyan would continuously lie about. She had begun to show signs of stress, and she couldn't risk anything going wrong with the baby, so she cut off all communication with Kiyan. At first he acted like he was cool with it, but as the months passed, he started to feel sick without Camara. He knew that he had been an asshole to her, and he had begun to regret his actions. All he wanted to do was right his wrongs with her and show her that he could be a good man to her. Kiyan tried to reach her on several occasions, but Camara continued to ignore him until the last month of her pregnancy. As she approached her due date, she allowed him to come back around.

"Damn, she looks just like me." Kiyan beamed as he stood over Camara. He had never experienced a love like this before. Everything about his baby girl was perfect, and he vowed to always protect her.

Camara just smiled, still exhausted from her day of pain. The nurses took the baby from Kiyan so they could weigh her and clean her up. Kiyan walked out to the family room to let everyone know that his baby girl had arrived.

His mother, Rochelle, Dinero, and Case were all seated in the room waiting.

"Aye, y'all, come on. She's here," Kiyan announced and then he led them into the room.

Everyone entered the room where Camara was holding the baby. She never wanted to let her go. The feeling Camara was experiencing was something she couldn't explain but she welcomed it with open arms.

Rochelle rushed over to the bed to see her new granddaughter.

"Kiy, she's beautiful. What's her name?" Rochelle asked, happy that she could share this experience with Kiyan.

"Milan Cheyenne DeMao," Kiyan told her.

Dinero walked next to Kiyan as he took a good look at the baby.

"Damn, this nigga is somebody's daddy now," Dinero joked.

"You better get your gun ready, bro. I can see all the little boys chasing her now," Case teased Kiyan.

"Man, please. You know I'm ready for that shit," he said, waving his hand dismissively.

"Aye, where Keece at?" Kiyan asked Dinero, noticing that he was missing.

"Keece and Big had to go to the Chi for some shit. They should be back soon," Dinero responded.

Case went to sit down on the recliner that was next to the bed.

"Did you call Pops at all?" Case asked Kiyan, hoping that they would settle their differences for the sake of the baby.

Rochelle looked up and gave Kiyan a worried look. She wasn't in the mood to be in Dom's presence, and she prayed that Kiyan hadn't called him to the hospital.

"Nah, I ain't even think to," Kiyan responded.

After Dom's attempted suicide, the boys' relationship with him still remained rocky. Keece and Dinero would speak to him sparingly, but it was nowhere near how it used to be before the drama. Big was the only one who talked to

Dom on a regular basis. Kiyan had lost a lot of respect for Dom, and he didn't feel like connecting with his father.

"Don't you think he would want to see his granddaughter?" Case asked, hoping Kiyan would reconsider his decision.

"He probably would, but I'm not thinking about him right now. I'm trying to enjoy *her*," Kiyan spat, looking at Milan in Rochelle's arms.

Case decided to drop the subject and let it go. He was tired of the division in his family. He just wanted it to end. Sometimes he felt like he was in the middle of the situation because whenever he was with his brothers, he couldn't talk about his parents. Whenever he would bring them up, the mood would shift and become very uncomfortable. Case knew his brothers had every reason to be upset, but he wished that they would talk it out and come to a resolution.

Kiyan knew Case was coming from a good place, but he wanted him to leave the situation alone for now. But Case had no understanding of how Kiyan, Dinero, and Keece had felt about not having their mother around. Kiyan had no plans of contacting his father anytime soon. He realized that six months without having contact with his father was bad, considering how close they once were, but he couldn't see himself having a conversation with him.

Kiyan walked over to Camara, who was propped up and trying to nurse their baby for the first time. To him, she never looked so beautiful. Her box braids were piled on top of her head in a bun, and her flawless bare skin glowed as if she had been in the sun for hours.

"You did good, girl," he said playfully, pinching her cheek.

"Shut up. I don't know if I'll ever do a natural birth again," she said softly, leaning her head back.

"Why not?" he quizzed.

"Because that was some bullshit. That pain was something that I've never felt before," she complained.

Kiyan brushed one of her braids out her face and then chuckled.

"Yeah, but she was worth it, right?" he asked.

Camara smiled as she looked down at her baby. "Yes, she was. I wish Paris would've made it, but she was tied up in court," she spoke with a sad face.

"I'm sure she'll come as soon as she lands," Kiyan said before kissing Camara on the forehead.

Kiyan was cooking up a plan in his head to get his woman back that he prayed would work. Seeing Camara bring his daughter into the world had sparked something within him. He hoped his plot for his family wouldn't backfire on him.

****

Keece sat on the passenger's side looking out of the window. He and Big had to meet up with one of their business associates in Chicago to make sure the operation was running smoothly. Life had been one big adjustment. Being without Paris for the last six months had been a hard pill to swallow for Keece. He missed everything about her and he wished that he could press rewind. He hadn't tried to contact Paris a single time because he was still salty about the way she'd ended their relationship. The fact that she had just written him out of her life had only upset him more.

Keece had finally lost hope in rekindling his relationship with Paris, and he had attempted to move on. He'd been carrying on like he wasn't affected by her departure, when the truth was he was lost without Paris. The fact that he had never gotten a chance to prove to her that he hadn't cheated on her left him feeling annoyed. If Paris was going to leave him, he wished it would've been for a valid reason and not because of speculation. Yes, he was wrong for going to Riley's house, but he hadn't gone over there with bad intentions. All he'd wanted to do was get his belongings. He never would've been stupid enough to stay the night at

Riley's house. However, from the outside looking in, it did look as though he had been up to no good. Now his pride was forcing him to live without the love of his life.

"So Camara and Kiyan had the baby?" Big asked, driving further into the city.

"Yeah. He just sent me some pictures. She looks just like his ass," Keece replied with a chuckle.

"That's *crazy*. That nigga done had a baby, and it's a *girl* at that. God must be tryin' to be funny." Big laughed.

Keece shook his head and then placed his phone in the cup holder.

"Hell yeah. I hope she drives his ass crazy too." He had to process that Kiyan's crazy ass was now a father. Keece always thought Dinero would be the next brother to have a baby since he was the ultimate ladies' man.

"You think he gon' let Pops see her?" Big asked.

Keece shrugged, not sure of what Kiyan's plans were when it came to that situation.

"I doubt it. He ain't trying to fuck with Pops like that. I mean, I know he's not feeling Pops like that, but I think we should all just work this shit out."

"I feel the same way, man. He really miss y'all coming around. He calls me all the time, trying to keep up with everybody and shit."

Keece just shook his head and began to roll a blunt. He didn't know why it was weighing on him to bury the hatchet with his father. It was time to put everything behind them, but he didn't know if Dinero and Kiyan were ready yet. Plus, he wanted to talk to his mother about it to get her take on the idea. Over the months, he and Rochelle had formed a strong bond, and Keece was excited that his mother was finally a part of his life. She had turned out to be cool, spunky, and down to earth. He felt comfortable around her and he wished he would've had more time with her when he was growing up.

"You still ain't heard from Paris?" Big asked, knowing the answer.

Keece shifted in his seat at the mention of her name. He hated talking about Paris because it caused him to miss her more.

"Hell nah. I ain't trippin', though. It is what it is," he said, fronting.

"Man, I don't blame you, especially if you ain't did shit. But that one bitch is a nice distraction, right?" Big smiled devilishly.

"Yeah, she's cool, but she a little clingy."

Keece had been seeing a woman by the name Alyssa for a couple months now. They had actually known each other for years since they had attended the same middle school.

Alyssa was a nice distraction from Paris for Keece, and she was fun to hang out with. But Keece knew deep down inside that he wouldn't be able to give Alyssa what she wanted.

"Alyssa is a fly lil' bitch, though. I used to want to fuck her in high school, but you know I couldn't pull that off with crazy-ass Tara on my back," Big said, referring to his baby mama.

Keece chuckled before he lit his blunt and inhaled the contents.

"Nah, she's cool as hell and got her own shit. I'm just not trying to do relationship type shit, especially with how shit ended with Paris. But I ain't gon' lie. I like her a lot."

"I feel you, though. I started fucking with Paris' little receptionist, Aimee. She's cool as shit."

Keece smiled, happy that Big had found someone he really liked.

"That's what's up. That's a good look for you."

"I know, but I gotta keep that shit on the low from Tara. I'm not trying to subject Aimee to her ignorant ass."

Keece shook his head at the thought of Tara. "I feel you, bro."

Keece was glad that he hadn't had children from a crazy bitch like Tara. At times, he felt bad for Big because he would have to deal with her forever, and she wasn't an easy person to get along with. Keece thought that she might have changed, but it had been years, and Tara showed no signs of evolving.

CHAPTER FIVE

Paris drove down the highway listening to Adrian Marcel's "Pieces". The lyrics seemed to be speaking to her soul as she sang along. Her life had changed drastically, forcing her to pick up the pieces of her life. A single tear escaped her eye as she reminisced about the days when she was happy. She would give *anything* just to feel that emotion again. Ever since Paris left Keece, she'd felt this void in her life that couldn't be filled. She always had a craving for his touch, his scent, and his love.

She missed him immensely, and she wished for things to be different. Keece had come into her life and made such an impact that she didn't think anyone would ever be able to capture her heart the way that he had. It pained her every day to wake up unable to see Keece lying next to her. Paris would force herself not to think about him, but there was no use when he resided in her mind as if he had signed a never-ending lease.

Although she longed for his presence, she wouldn't allow herself to cave into being back with him. Every time she thought about his infidelity, it caused her heart to ache. She didn't know if she could ever get over him backtracking to Riley. After all, considering the heartache that Riley had caused Keece, Paris couldn't understand the reason why he had maintained contact with her. The fact that he had spent the night with her still ate Paris up inside.

Since leaving Keece, her professional career had bloomed. Paris now had her own law firm in downtown Milwaukee. She loved being on her own and not having to take orders from anybody. Her receptionist, Aimee, had ended up coming with her, and Paris couldn't have been happier. Paris had more clients than ever, since people were referring her from her old firm.

She walked into her office and was greeted by Aimee, who had become a close friend during the last couple of months. She was easy to talk to and a great companion to have.

"Hey, girl, the phone has been blowing up all day. New clients are calling, so your schedule next week is packed. You also have three messages," Aimee said, handing her some documents.

Paris looked through the papers briefly. "Thank you, Aimee. Oh, I almost forgot. How was your date with *Big*?"

Aimee smiled coyly before speaking. "It was nice. I really like him for some reason. He's got this cool vibe, and I'm kinda digging it."

"To be honest, you're fucking with a real dude. I like Big."

"Me too."

Paris had given Big Aimee's number as promised, and the two had hit it off well. After talking for months, they had finally gone on their first date. Paris wanted to warn Aimee about Big's baby mama, but she didn't want to plant any negative seeds. So she would just allow her to figure it out for herself.

Paris sat down in her office chair and logged on to her computer. As soon as she began to check her emails, her cell rang. She looked at the caller ID and smiled. She had begun dating a guy named Chase a few months ago, and while she was determined that they wouldn't get involved too deeply, she still enjoyed his conversation.

"Hello?" she answered as she swiveled in her office chair.

"What's up, lil mama? You busy?" his deep baritone asked.

"Um...not yet. I just got to the office. Why? What's up?"

"Nothing. I want to see you today if possible."

Paris smiled, liking the idea of seeing him again.

"I'm sure I can squeeze you in today. I'm surprise you're not busy, considering its Friday, and I know everybody's trying to get their cars in before the weekend. ."

Chase was a manager for an auto shop on the north side of Milwaukee. Word around town was that he was one of the best mechanics the Mil had ever seen.

"Nah, I've been busy as fuck, but I'm trying to get done early so I can see you."

"Well, I'll call you when I get off, and then we could meet somewhere. Is that cool?" she asked him.

"Yeah, just hit my line."

"Bye."

Paris had met Chase while shopping with Camara. He had approached her like a gentleman, and Paris was very intrigued by him. It also didn't help that he was one of the sexiest men she'd ever seen. Now he wasn't better looking than *Keece*, but he was still fine. He stood around six feet even with flawless brown skin. He had almond shaped eyes, a slender nose, and kissable lips. Chase had no facial hair, which gave him a youthful look. His body was nice and tight with muscles bulging everywhere. After exchanging numbers, they began communicating on a daily basis.

Seconds later, Aimee walked into her office. "Here are the files from yesterday," she said, giving Paris more documents and folders.

"Guess who just called me?" Paris asked excitedly.

"Who?" Aimee quizzed.

Paris smiled. "Chase. He wants to meet up somewhere after work."

Aimee crossed her arms under her breasts and gave Paris a smirk. "Ooh, it seems like somebody likes him, but I just have to ask; are you really over Keece?"

Paris ran her fingers through her hair and released a sigh. She would be lying if she said that she was totally over Keece. Although she thought of him day and night, Paris wasn't ready to run back into his arms at that moment.

"Honestly, I don't know. I really miss my baby, but he fucked up, and now I have to move on. Now, I'm not trying to get serious with Chase because I still love Keece, but it's nice to have some male company."

"Yeah, I guess it is, but secretly, I'm still rooting for you and Keece to get back together."

Paris rolled her eyes playfully. "Yeah, you and everybody else is too."

Everyone from her mama down to Camara wanted her and Keece to get back together, but Paris wasn't feeling it.

She was still hurt and she didn't see it going away anytime soon. Paris knew if she were to see Keece face to face, it would be a different story since she was still weak for him. That's why she chose to stay away from him, so he wouldn't pull her back under his spell.

****

It was finally time for Camara and the baby to be released from the hospital, and she couldn't have been more excited. She missed her bed terribly, and the food that they'd been serving her should've been outlawed by the government. Kiyan carefully secured baby Milan in her car seat while the nurse helped Camara get comfortable in wheelchair. After gathering their belongings, they went to the car where they got strapped in and pulled off.

Kiyan had purchased a four bedroom home not too far from Keece's house. Seeing his daughter being birthed into the world had opened Kiyan's eyes more than ever before. He no longer wanted to play the field and fuck random girls. He was now someone's father, and he wanted to be a good example for Milan and show her what a man was supposed to be. He also wanted to be a good man to Camara because she deserved it. She had put up with all of his bullshit for the past two years, and he knew a woman like her wouldn't be single for long. Plus he didn't want another man around Milan.

Kiyan pulled up to the colonial style home and put the car in park.

"Who's house is this?" Camara asked.

"It's *ours.* I want us to live here together," he said, looking deeply into her eyes.

Camara smiled nervously. "Kiyan, stop playing." She chuckled as she waved her hand dismissively.

"Nah, I'm serious. I really wanna work this shit out, Camara. I want our baby to be raised in the same household and not have to live between two different homes. I love you, and I'm sorry for all the shit I've put you through. But witnessing Milan's birth changed me. I know you're a good woman, and you deserve the world. I promise I'm going to give it to you if you give me another chance. No more bitches and no more lies. This time I'm trying to do right by y'all. So are you gon' give a nigga another chance?" Kiyan asked, smiling, but on the inside he was nervous.

Camara couldn't stop the tears from falling down if she wanted to. This was what she had wanted for so long, and to hear Kiyan finally speak the words made her so happy. She too didn't want to raise their daughter in separate households. She was glad that Kiyan had finally stepped up and made a decision that would benefit them all.

"You know I love you, Kiyan. Listen, I'll give you another chance as long as you promise to take care of my heart and not play with my emotions."

"I promise I'm not on that shit no more. Now give me a kiss," he demanded.

Camara took his face into her hands and kissed him passionately. They made love to each other's mouths briefly before breaking away. Kiyan got out and opened the door for Camara, grabbed the baby, and walked them inside of their new home. The house was beautiful with an arched opening and big bay windows. The decorative ceilings highlighted the great room. The kitchen was huge with stainless steel appliances and a breakfast nook. Each bedroom had its own bathroom, and the master suite was equipped with two huge walk-in closets and a balcony. Kiyan hadn't had time to decorate the entire house, but he'd made sure that their bedroom was furnished, as well as Milan's nursery.

"Kiyan, this house is amazing. I love it," Camara gushed.

"I knew you would. You can decorate the rest of it however you like. But as for my man cave, I need that shit to look cold. I don't want none of that Martha Stewart type shit."

Camara hit him playfully. "Shut up. You know I've got good taste," she said rolling her eyes.

Kiyan laughed. "I know. I'm just fucking with you. Look, my mom is going to come over and stay to help us out with the baby for a while, so make sure she feels comfortable. A'ight?"

Camara looked at him and simply nodded. Kiyan had left Camara speechless with his kind words and the new house. She had never felt happier in her life. "I love you so much. Thank you for this," she told him, wrapping her arms around his neck.

"I love you too. Now get some rest while the baby is asleep, and I'll be back later."

Kiyan kissed her before he left. Camara couldn't wait to call Paris and update her on her unexpected love life. She knew her friend would be happy for her since she had always cheered for her and Kiyan to get back together.

****

Paris checked her appearance in the rearview mirror after pulling up to the restaurant. She was about to meet Chase for dinner, and she wanted to make sure her look was on point. She got out of her car and walked inside of the restaurant. Spotting Chase at the bar, she walked over and tapped him on the shoulder. He turned around and licked his lips. Paris was looking good in a black long sleeve crop top, a high-waist skirt with zipper detailing, and black fringe high heel sandals. Her hair was styled bone straight with a part down the middle and her makeup was applied lightly.

"Hey you," she said, giving him a hug.

"What's up, P?" he replied with the nickname he had given her.

"Are we eating at the bar or getting a table?"

Chase shook his head and stood, towering over her.

"Nah, I got us a table over there. Come on."

Chase grabbed her hand and led her over to a booth near the bar. After looking over the menu and giving the waiter their orders, they sparked up a conversation.

"You look good tonight, Ms. Parker," he smirked.

She smiled coyly. "Thank you. I try."

"I'm glad you agreed to have dinner with me. I think the last time I saw you was about a week ago."

Paris stirred her drink. "I know. I've been so busy at work that I haven't had much time to play. I'm sure you found other things to do. I know I'm not the only woman you talk to," she teased.

"No, you're not the only female I talk to, but you're the only one I'm interested in," Chase said, licking his lips.

Paris could've sworn she felt her kitty throb. "Oh really?"

"For real. I'm feeling you like crazy, but I know you just got out of a relationship. So I'm not trying to rush you. By the way, you never told me what happened between you and your ex."

Paris thought for a moment before she answered his question. She didn't feel like discussing what had gone down between her and Keece. She just didn't feel like opening up that bottle of feelings that she'd tried so desperately to keep away.

"I don't wanna get into that. It's a long story. I want to be honest with you. I'm not ready for a relationship right now. Now I'm not saying that it's not a possibility that we couldn't grow into something more serious later on. But right now I'm not looking for a commitment," she revealed.

Chase was a little hurt by her revelation, but he didn't express it. He knew that she'd had a bad break up with her ex, and maybe she wasn't over him, but Chase didn't care. She was special, and he had big plans for Paris. So he was willing to wait as long as she needed him to.

Chase sat back in his seat. "That's cool, P. I'm not trying to rush you into anything. I just want you to know that I'll wait as long as you need me to, okay?"

"Okay."

Paris and Chase continued to converse over dinner. She loved his company, and she had to admit that he was a nice substitute for Keece. Most days, her thoughts were consumed with Keece and what they used to share, but whenever she was with Chase, he made her forget all about her heartbreak.

After dinner, the couple sat in Chase's car and talked for hours about life, kids, and their careers. Paris found it interesting that Chase had wanted to open a community center instead of an auto shop. He'd explained that he had a passion for helping out troubled kids and wouldn't mind being a mentor. After their talk, they parted ways and promised to get together soon.

The following day, Paris sat in Camara's bedroom and raved about how gorgeous baby Milan was. She couldn't help but wonder how her and Keece's baby would've looked if they'd had one together. She'd wanted so badly to bear his first child and share his last name, but their current circumstances had prevented her from doing so.

"Cammy, can I please have her? She is so damn cute," Paris said as she kissed the baby's cheeks.

Camara cut her eyes at Paris while folding her laundry. "Hell no! That's my little pumpkin right there. Besides, you wouldn't be able to get past her daddy. He is in love with her."

"I bet he is. I'm so happy y'all worked out your issues. You're probably the only one who knows how to handle Kiyan," Paris teased.

Camara gave her a knowing look. "I know right? He is a piece of work. But for real, though, I'm glad he finally stepped up and realized that I love him and got his back like no other bitch. He's really trying to be a good man," Camara said with a smile.

"I'm glad *somebody* got their happy ending. You make me believe that true love can be found even after all the bullshit."

Camara smacked her lips and rolled her eyes at Paris' dramatic ass. "Girl, stop playing. You know your true love is Keece. I know you think he cheated on you, but have you ever thought that maybe he didn't. I never took Keece as the type of man who cheats. He's a loyal guy. You need to quit playing and get your man back. The new chick he's with ain't the deal."

Paris snapped her neck at Camara. She hoped what she'd just heard was just a joke.

"What new chick? He got a new bitch already?" Paris quipped, feeling like her heart would explode. She wasn't ready to hear that Keece had moved on with another woman.

"It's some chick named Alyssa. Kiyan is actually the one that told me about her. I've never seen her. Why do you care? You don't want him. *And* you're with that one dude," Camara challenged.

Paris gave her a dirty look. "What do you mean why do I care? That's my fucking baby, even though he was on that bullshit. Now you got me all in my feelings with this shit."

Paris handed the baby to Camara and started pacing the floor.

Did I do too much by not letting him tell his side of the story? Should I have left the way that I did? Is it too late for us when he has a new girlfriend? Paris' mind began to race as the questions started to arise. Yes, she was talking to someone new, but she didn't want Keece to move on. Paris didn't want to see him giving away all of the love she should've been getting to some other woman.

Moments later, there was knock on the door.

"Hey, you want me to take her?" Rochelle asked, stepping inside the bedroom. She had been there for two weeks now, and Camara was so thankful for her help.

"Sure. Oh, I'm sorry, Rochelle. This is my best friend, Paris. Paris, this is Kiyan's mom, Rochelle."

"His *mom*? Wow! You're pretty. It's nice to meet you."

Rochelle smiled, shaking her hand. "You are too, sweetie."

Rochelle grabbed the baby and walked out. Paris couldn't get over how young Rochelle looked. For her to have three grown sons, she didn't look a day over forty. She'd had no idea that Keece's mother was back in his life. It seemed like so much had happened since she and Keece separated.

"So you have to tell me the details. Where the hell did *she* come from? Was she in jail or on drugs? What it is?" Paris asked, rambling question after question.

"Damn, girl, calm down with all of the damn questions," Camara snapped.

Camara then went on to explain how Rochelle had come back into the boys lives. Camara even informed her of Keece's status in the drug business after much reluctance. Paris' mouth fell wide open when Camara informed her of the roles that Dom and Celine had played in Rochelle's disappearance. Paris had never taken Dom and Celine as people who would do something so callous.

"Dom and Celine ain't shit! Why would you hurt your children like that? That's fucked up," Paris spat, after taking a sip of water.

"Girl, I said the same thing. Kiyan hasn't talked to his father since he tried to commit suicide."

Paris spit the water out all over the floor. She'd had no idea that Dom had tried to kill himself. "What the fuck? I didn't know any of this shit. Where the fuck have I been? How come you ain't tell me this shit?"

"I didn't know until recently. Don't forget I wasn't fucking with Kiyan during my pregnancy. And if your ass spit on my damn floor again, I'm kicking your ass out," Camara threatened.

Paris rolled her eyes and waved her hand. "So, remember when I asked you about Keece's extracurricular activities, and you acted like you didn't know anything? Yeah, you ain't loyal, hoe." Paris shook her head.

Camara pretended to pout as she crawled over to Paris who was sitting on the bed. Paris pushed her away as she tried to hug and kiss her.

"Nah, get your lying ass off of me!" Paris yelled as she tried to dodge Camara.

"I'm sorry, honey. Kiyan made me promise not to tell anyone. I couldn't say anything at the time. Please forgive me," she pleaded.

"Get off of me," Paris said with a smirk.

"I know. I'm such a bad friend." Camara giggled and then went back to folding clothes.

Paris rolled her eyes at her. "No, you're a *bitch*, but let's get back to their mother. She's got it going on."

"I know. She does look young, right? She's cool as hell too. I'm kind of happy she decided to stay here so Milan can have both of her granny's in her life." Camara beamed.

"Oh, so she moved up here?"

"Yep. The boys are actually in the process of buying her a house. They've been taking really good care of her. You can tell that they had missed their mother being around."

"I guess that's good," Paris said somberly as she laid back on the bed.

"Now don't be getting all depressed and shit. You know Keece still loves you, but Paris, you were the one being stubborn and told him that you didn't want him anymore. What was he supposed to do? Just wait for you to come around and not move on? You can't have it both ways, boo. If you want him back, just call and talk to him. I know you've been raving about how nice this new guy is, but be for real, that nigga don't do it for you like Keece does."

Paris huffed. "No, he doesn't, but he does take my mind off of Keece. I don't know about shit no more. Your ass threw me off my square telling me he had a new bitch," Paris complained.

KEECE AND PARIS 2

"Well, I didn't want you to run into them somewhere and find out that way."

Paris was really confused now that she knew there was a new leading lady in Keece's life. The jealousy was seeping into her pores as she thought about Keece being intimate with the woman. Although she hadn't been intimate with Chase, she now thought that maybe she was holding back for nothing. Keece was for sure having sex with his new girlfriend, so why shouldn't Paris have a little fun too?

Now my day is all fucked up.

CHAPTER SIX

Keece bit his bottom lip and moaned lightly as he was being pleasured. Alyssa had been giving him mind-blowing head for the last ten minutes, and he was about to explode. He stood leaning against the wall for support trying not to buckle his knees. Keece gripped the back of her head as she bobbed up and down on his shaft. Alyssa gave the best head known to mankind, and Keece couldn't get enough of it.

Minutes later, he erupted inside of her mouth, and she swallowed every drop. Alyssa smiled as she stood up and went to the bathroom to brush her teeth. Keece gathered himself together and pulled up his pants.

"So what's on your agenda today?" Alyssa asked, coming back into the bedroom.

Alyssa was considered beautiful, standing at 5'2" with a thick physique. She wore her hair in long extensions, and she had skin the color of chocolate. Her light brown eyes, perfect nose, and pouty lips completed her cute face.

"I gotta go see my niece today. She was born a couple weeks ago," he told her, checking his phone.

"Which brother had the baby?"

"Kiyan."

"Oh, well, will I see you again tonight?"

Keece looked up at her. "You want to?" he asked, giving her his signature smirk.

"Of course I do. I always wanna spend more time with you," she purred, walking up to him and wrapping her arms around his neck.

"A'ight. Be ready at eight o'clock. I'll take you out tonight."

"Really?" she asked excitedly.

"Yeah. Wear something sexy...something with some easy access." Then he laughed and walked out.

He walked out of her house and jumped in his car. Keece knew that Alyssa may have caught feelings for him, and that kind of scared him a bit. He had stressed to her that he didn't want a relationship, but at times Alyssa was hard to resist. Plus, she kept his mind off of Paris, and he appreciated that.

After a twenty minute ride, Keece pulled up to Kiyan's home and got out. He rang the doorbell and was greeted by Camara.

"Hey, Keece, how're you doing?" she asked, hugging him.

"I'm good. I came to see the baby."

Camara pointed. "Oh, she's in the family room with your mom."

Keece walked to the family room where he saw Kiyan and Dinero playing 2K while his mother fed the baby.

"What is your ass doing here?" Kiyan asked greeting him.

Keece walked past Kiyan to get to the couch. "I came to see the baby, nigga. Dinero, I called your ugly ass last night, Why you ain't answer?" Keece questioned him.

Dinero chuckled with eyes fixated on the TV. "Oh, my bad... I was with this one bitch. What did you need?"

"Nothing now." Keece sat by his mother and watched her feed Milan. Keece had never seen a baby so pretty in his life, and he was happy that she was a part of his family tree.

"This is a cute-ass baby. I don't know how she ended up being your daughter, though," Keece joked.

Dinero joined in. "It's only because of Camara, not his ugly ass."

Kiyan gave both of his brothers a mean mug. "Fuck both of you bitches," he spat.

"Y'all act like your mother isn't sitting here. Learn some respect," Rochelle scolded them.

"My bad, Mama," Kiyan apologized.

Rochelle turned toward Keece. "So I finally met the woman who stole my son's heart," she sang.

Keece raised his eyebrows, wondering who she was referring to. "Who are you talking about?"

"Nigga, you know who she's talking about. *Paris*!" Dinero jumped in.

"Keece, she is beautiful. I see why you're still in love with her," Rochelle gushed.

"Paris was *here*?" Keece asked, surprised that she had finally shown her face.

Kiyan nodded while sipping on a soda. "Yeah. She came to see Milan a couple days ago. Why did you ask? I thought your ass was over her," he challenged.

Keece sucked his teeth. "I never told you that. I told you I was done chasing her ass," he corrected him.

"It's all the same thing. You know you still want her," Dinero added.

"How did this conversation end up on me and Paris? Both of you niggas need to mind your own business 'cause, Kiyan, you just got in good with Camara," Keece snapped.

Kiyan paused the game and looked at Keece. "I know, and I'm trying to keep it that way. If me and Camara can work it out, then it's still hope for you and Paris," he said confidently.

"Look, baby, I can tell that you still love her, so why don't you try one more time? If she rejects you, then you can move on and never look back. When she was here, I heard her and Camara talking. She's not over you, but she is still hurt by what she *thinks* went down. I think if you explain to her what really happened between you and Riley, you'll be all good. Plus, you need to get on it because she's been seeing another man."

Dinero laughed. "*Damn*! How do you know all of that? You're nosy as hell, Mama."

She laughed too. "Call it what you want."

Keece pondered on what he'd just been told. It burned him up to hear that Paris was seeing someone new.

"I'm really not trying to go back down that road with Paris. I think we should remain in the place where we are," Keece said.

"You sure?" Kiyan asked, knowing his brother was putting on a front.

Keece simply nodded his head, hoping he could live by the words he had just spoken. He was still stuck on the fact that Paris was seeing someone else. The thought of another man touching her caused steam to shoot out of his ears. He knew he couldn't fathom seeing Paris ride off into the sunset with another man, but he had no other choice but to accept it.

CHAPTER SEVEN

Celine sat at the bar downing her fourth shot of the night. Ever since Dom said he wanted a divorce, alcohol seemed to be her beverage of choice. She had tried on numerous occasions to reach out to him, but he was never available. She couldn't see the rest of her days without Dom. She wished that she could get an hour of his time just to ask for his forgiveness. The only person she seemed to have in her corner was Case, but even he got tired of her calling just to hear her cry. Celine didn't want to be a burden to her baby boy, but she had no one else. She had come from a small family, and they had lived miles away in Hawaii. She didn't even have the courage to call her mother to tell her about her dilemma.

After ordering another shot, Celine noticed Rochelle walk in with another woman in tow. Celine couldn't help but be jealous of her chipper appearance. Her skin radiated under the dim lights. Her hair was styled in a fresh wrap, and her outfit was on point. Rochelle had always been beautiful, but Celine had been too jealous to admit it.

Feeling the effects of the liquor, she stood up and stumbled toward Rochelle.

"So, you win again, Rochelle," Celine slurred as she approached her.

Rochelle looked over to her right and rolled her eyes to the ceiling. She couldn't believe Celine had the balls to step to her after the painful things she'd done. Rochelle had been itching to knock her ass out anyhow.

"This miserable bitch," Rochelle said to her cousin, Tee, who chuckled at the remark.

Celine drunkenly leaned on the bar for support. "You happy now, huh? Once again you have me looking like a fool," she ranted.

"Dom must've left your dumbass, huh?" Rochelle smirked before ordering her drink.

Celine narrowed her eyes at her. "No, he didn't! We're actually doing quite well, in fact," she lied.

Rochelle smacked her lips. "Bitch, please! Who do you think you're fooling? That nigga don't fuck with your trifling ass, and he shouldn't. Well, I take that back. Both of you miserable bitches deserve each other."

"Why are you so mad that I stepped up and took care of your man and sons?" Celine smirked, hitting below the belt.

"Chelle, let me fuck this skinny bitch up!" Tee said, getting riled up.

Rochelle grabbed Tee's arm, gesturing for her to take a seat. "Nah, I got it."

"You see Celine, you're just mad that you'll never be me," Rochelle spat, getting into Celine's face. "You wanted to be me so bad that why you stole my man and even tried to raise my sons. In your mind, you actually thought that you were filling Rochelle's shoes. But the truth is you were just a carbon copy of me. Dom didn't look at you the way he looked at me. He didn't touch you the way that he touched me, and he damn sure didn't fuck you the way that he fucked me. That's why I ended up giving him *three* sons and your spoiled belly ass only gave him *one*. So do me and yourself a favor, and get the fuck out of my face before I beat your ass."

Celine's chest heaved up and down as she glared at Rochelle. "You bitch!" she screamed.

Without warning, Rochelle grabbed the drink she'd been sipping on and threw it in Celine's face. Celine tried desperately to wipe the alcohol from her face to soothe her burning eyes. Rochelle threw a right punch and then a left one, causing Celine to fall over one of the bar stools. Before

Rochelle could finish her off, the security guard came and stopped her.

"Talk that shit now, hoe!" Rochelle yelled, trying to free herself from the guard's strong grasp.

Celine tried to jump back up quickly, but the other guard grabbed her too. She hated that Rochelle had gotten the best of her.

"This shit ain't over, Rochelle!" Celine yelled, pointing her finger.

"I know, bitch," Rochelle spat. "I'll see your funky ass again."

Since Celine was still belligerent and visibly drunk, she was carried out of the bar while Rochelle retook her seat next to Tee. It felt so good to have finally kicked Celine's ass. She had waited years to get her hands on her and the experience was everything she'd imagined it would be. Rochelle turned to Tee and stared at her for a moment before they both broke out into laughter

"Let's toast to whooping that hoe's ass!" Tee laughed

****

Paris and Aimee had just walked into of the movie theater in Menomonee Falls. Since their work day had ended early, they decided to catch a movie together. After buying their tickets, Paris and Aimee made their way to the concession stand. While Aimee placed her order, Paris noticed a familiar person walking out of one of the theaters. Instantly, her breathing became shallow as her heart began to palpitate. Keece walked out with his arm wrapped around a woman's neck. His curly box had grown a little longer, and had been lined to perfection. Keece's goatee had now grown into a full beard, which gave him a rugged appearance. Paris' heart pounded just at the sight of him. He still was the most handsome man she'd ever been with. She could feel the envy invade her insides as she watched Keece smile in the woman's face.

He used to look at me that way, Paris thought to herself.

"Look who's here," Paris whispered to Aimee.

Aimee looked over and gasped lightly. She could tell by the look on Paris' face that she was bothered by seeing Keece with another woman.

"I should go say hi," Paris said and walked off without hearing a response from Aimee.

She strutted over still dressed in her work attire and made sure to smooth down her hair. She could feel her chest tighten as nervousness took over her body. She tapped Keece's shoulder and then waited anxiously for his reaction.

"Hey you!" she spoke with a smug smirk on her face as Keece turned around.

He was shocked to see Paris and even more so that she had actually come over to speak to him. She still looked as beautiful as he had remembered, but only now she had blonde highlights sprinkled through her hair. A piece of Keece wanted to scoop her up into his arms and kiss her juicy lips, but he was still salty over the way she had abruptly ended their relationship.

"Hey, Paris. What's up?" Keece asked calmly, with his arm still wrapped around Alyssa.

Alyssa gave Paris a friendly look while she waited for her response.

Paris shifted on her leg, "Just here to see a movie. How've you been?"

"I'm good, but aye, I gotta go. We have somewhere else to be. I'll see you around," he said and then walked out hand in hand with Alyssa.

Paris could almost feel the tears gather in her eyes as she watched Keece walk out with his new girlfriend. She couldn't believe how he had just blown her off like they had never been together. A part of her wanted to chase after him and curse him out, but she quickly decided against it. Paris didn't want to embarrass herself over Keece.

"So what did he say?" Aimee asked, walking over to where she stood.

Paris smacked her lips and snorted. "Girl, I don't even wanna talk about it. Let's go watch this movie," she said, walking away.

Keece, on the other hand, was smiling on the inside at his blunt attitude. He knew it may have been childish, but he couldn't help it. It made him happy to see Paris so jealous of Alyssa. She needed to see that Keece wasn't some square who would sit waiting for her to come around. Although it had satisfied him, a part of Keece felt like he may have gone overboard.

"Babe, who was that woman?" Alyssa asked when they got inside of the car.

"That was my ex," he said, cranking up the engine.

"Oh... she's pretty. Why did y'all breakup?"

Keece paused for a moment. "Long story," he finally responded, shutting down the possibility of opening up the topic.

Alyssa brushed off the subject since Keece seemed as if he didn't want to talk about it. She figured there was no need to worry about the last chick if she was there with him at the moment. Plus, she and Keece were having such a good day that she didn't want to spoil it by bringing up his ex.

CHAPTER EIGHT

"So he basically shitted on you?" Camara asked.

"Hell yeah! Fuck him, though," Paris said, filling Camara in on her encounter with Keece over the phone.

"So how did the girl look? Was she cute?"

Paris perched her lips up before responding, "She was. In fact, she was *beautiful*. I guess I can say Keece has good taste."

Camara sucked her teeth. "Do you see what your stubbornness has caused? Now ya man is parading around with another woman on his arm," she fussed, which caused Paris to smack her lips.

"You swear Keece didn't do shit, right? You do remember him staying out all night with his ex, or did you forget?"

"Yeah, I remember, but I don't think he spent the night with that girl. I believe him when said spent the night in his car," Camara said a matter-of-factly.

"Whatever... We shouldn't even be talking about the enemy. I should be preparing for my date with Chase."

"Hmm...sounds like fun. Well, have a ball and use a condom. Bye," Camara said and hung up.

Paris shook her head and began to get dressed. Chase had invited her over because he was going to cook a meal for her. She'd finally decided to let her guard down with him and let whatever was meant to be happen. After seeing that Keece had moved on, it had prompted Paris to do the same. This would be the first time that she would visit Chase's home. Whenever they'd seen each other previously, it had been in a public setting. Since they would be chilling at Chase's home, Paris threw on some casual but chic clothing.

After checking her hair and makeup, she received a text from Chase telling her that he was outside.

Paris exited her home and spotted Chase standing on the passenger's side with the door open. He was looking quite handsome with his fresh line up and million dollar smile.

"What's up, Ms. Parker?" he asked, giving her a hug and a peck on the lips.

"Hi Chase," Paris responded coyly while getting inside of the car.

Chase walked around to the driver's side and hopped in. He turned down his music and looked over at Paris. "Damn, you finally let a nigga pick you up. I just knew you was gon' say you would meet me there." He laughed.

Paris chuckled. "I had to make sure you weren't some crazy person. I don't like people to know where I lay my head."

"I feel you. Well, sit back and enjoy the night I have prepared for you."

"Cool."

Chase pulled off and began driving. For the most part, the ride was quiet while J. Cole flowed through the speakers. Thirty minutes later, they pulled up to a nice two-level home with a wraparound porch.

"Come on," Chase instructed Paris.

Paris got out and walked over to Chase, who grabbed her hand and led her inside of the house. She looked around and silently approved. It was very neat and clean with modern décor. There wasn't a lot of furniture, only the bare minimum.

"Your house is nice," she complimented, looking at the artwork on the wall.

Chase turned and looked at her. "Oh, this isn't my house. My cousin actually lives here. I'm just house-sitting for him."

"Oh, okay," she replied, feeling odd that he would bring her to someone else's house.

Chase led Paris into the kitchen where there was a medium sized table decorated with a tablecloth and a candle in the center. Paris smiled at the gesture and sat in her chair. Chase then walked over to the oven where he pulled out two plates topped with a steak, baked potato and broccoli. Paris rubbed her hands together as thoughts of devouring her food came into play.

"This looks good, Chase. Did you really cook this?" she asked teasingly

Chase gave her a funny look. "Yeah, girl. That'll be the best food you've ever tasted in your life," he bragged.

"Yeah...okay," she replied sarcastically.

Paris bit into her food and allowed the taste to marinate in her mouth. She couldn't deny that Chase had done a good job cooking.

While eating, the couple began to converse about different subjects. The more time Paris spent around Chase, the more comfortable she became. Sometimes when she allowed her mind to run free, she could see herself getting serious with him. She loved that he was attentive, caring, and didn't mind sharing his feelings.

"I'm full," Paris declared, rubbing her stomach.

"Me too. Let's go watch something," he suggested.

Chase led her to the TV room where he turned on the television. They sat next to each other on the sofa. Chase surfed the TV Guide channel trying to find something that they both would enjoy.

"What kind of movies you like?" he asked.

Paris shrugged. "I can pretty much watch anything. It doesn't matter."

"Well, I've got some bootleg movies. I'll be right back," he said and then left the room.

Paris still felt eerie about being in someone else's home. She didn't understand why Chase hadn't taken her to his home instead of his cousin's. Paris couldn't get fully comfortable because she was nervous about someone else walking in.

Chase returned to the room, saying, "Okay, I've got Straight Outta Compton and The Perfect Stranger. Which one?"

"Let's do The Perfect Stranger."

"A'ight. Cool. You want something to drink?"

"Sure. I'll take water."

Chase left and returned with a bottle of water. Paris took the bottle and opened it, but she noticed that the seal had been broken. She held the bottle of water in the air.

"Um...can I get a bottle that hasn't been opened?"

Chase gave her a puzzled look. "What do you mean?"

"The seal is broken on this bottle."

Chase took the bottle and examined it before putting it back on the table. He left the room again. While the bottle sat on the table, Paris noticed a white substance settling at the bottom of it.

What the fuck is that? Paris thought.

Instantly, her guard went up and a bit of panic consumed her body. She grabbed her purse and pulled out her phone. Just as she started texting Camara, Chase returned to the room with more water. It wasn't in a bottle this time. He had poured some in a cup.

"This should be cool," he said, handing her the cup.

Paris examined the cup and observed the same white substance. This time it was floating at the top of the water. She realized that Chase was on some sneaky shit. Paris was baffled to say the least. What were the odds that the same white substance would be floating through the bottle as well as the cup?

Okay, Paris, think. Don't let him know that you're on to him, she coached herself.

"You know what? My secretary just texted me and said that she has a flat tire. I'm sorry, but I'm going to have to cut the night short," she said with a fake pout.

"She doesn't have anyone else she can call?" Chase questioned.

Paris shook her head. "No, she doesn't have any family here, and I don't wanna leave her hanging like that," she lied.

Chase sat as though he was in deep thought. It was as if he'd zoned out while Paris sat there wondering what the hell his problem was.

"Um...hello? Earth to Chase. Could you take me back to my car?" she asked, breaking him from his thoughts.

Chase blinked a few times before replying to her. "Ah...Yeah... Well, how about I take you to pick her up? Would that work?"

Paris shook her head quickly. She didn't want him anywhere near her, despite her calm demeanor. She would continue to play nice to ensure that he wouldn't do anything crazy.

"No, that's okay. I wouldn't want to be a burden, and besides, I have Triple A."

"It's really not a problem, Paris," Chase persisted.

Becoming irritated with his insistence, Paris huffed. She knew he was on some sneaky shit just by the way the conversation was going. She needed to get away from him in a hurry.

"Chase, I don't need your help. Now can you take me to my car?" she asked and stood up.

Paris grabbed her belongings and tried to walk around Chase, but he grabbed her arm and pushed her back.

"You ain't going no fucking where," he said with a cold demeanor as she fell down on the couch. "Now sit your ass down!"

Paris was scared to death as he stood over her with a menacing glare. She tried to get back up, but he pushed her down again. Fear began to set in her body as she thought of ways to get out of the house. She would've never thought she would be in this predicament with Chase of all people.

"What the fuck? Why are you doing this? Just please let me go," Paris tried to reason with him.

Chase bent down and caressed her face softly. "Listen, baby, I'm about to get a lot of money for you. So just sit back and chill," he said with a crooked grin on his face.

"Money for me? What the hell are you talking about?" she asked in a panic.

"Yeah. Your new owner should be here tomorrow. I wish I could keep you for myself, but this nigga about to give me twenty stacks for you, and I can't afford to pass that money up."

Paris' mouth fell open as she tried to process what Chase had just said. Was he really trying to sell her as if she was a Barbie doll at the toy store?

"What the fuck? I'm getting out of here!" she announced.

Paris hopped up and tried to run to the front door. Chase grabbed her by her ponytail and yanked her back, causing her to fall to the floor. Paris could feel all of the wind leaving her body as she tried to gasp for air. Chase stood over her with a wicked look on his face and punched her in the face, causing Paris to see black instantly.

****

Keece and Big sat outside of the House of Corrections center waiting on Big's sister, Danica, to be released. She'd been arrested the night before, so Big had to bail her out. Danica was a constant headache for Big, but he wouldn't dare leave his little sister in jail, even though she had done wrong.

"Danica's ass needs some anger management treatment," Keece told Big.

"Nah, she needs somebody to beat her ass real good. She thinks she can whoop everybody," Big responded, taking a pull from the blunt.

"You know sometimes I think about stepping out of the game, bro," Keece revealed to Big.

Big choked on the blunt after hearing Keece's revelation. After minutes of trying to catch his breath, he looked over at Keece who was laughing hysterically.

"Keece, what the fuck you talking about? You gon' give all of this shit up for what?" Big inquired, hoping this was just a phase.

"I was thinking about getting back into tattooing and maybe open up a couple of shops and build a franchise."

Big nodded, liking the sound of his idea. "You used to be cold with that shit too."

Keece used to be a tattoo artist long before he was selected to take over his family's business. He missed doing it and he wanted to open up his own shop. In fact, he had done all of his brothers' tats and some of his own. He didn't know how Kiyan and Dinero would take it, but the idea had been on his mind for a long time.

"This shit ain't fun like it used to be. I think I've outgrown the thrill of the game, to be honest. Maybe you and Kiyan could take over. I trust y'all to make the right decisions, and I think Pops would too."

"What about Dinero?" Big asked.

Keece shook his head. "Nah, Dinero ain't ready for that kind of power yet."

"Damn, Keece, you gon' do lil bro' like that? That nigga gon' be salty for real," Big stressed.

"He will, but you saw that shit he pulled with that Dyno situation. I know it led us to my mama, but that was a huge fuck up. He got played way too easy, even after we had all agreed that it wouldn't be the best move for us. He still went ahead and did the shit. I'm not saying he's not equipped to be in charge. I just feel that he's not ready now."

Keece knew Dinero would be upset by his decision, but he had suffered no consequences when he made the decision to do business with Dyno. Not to mention the murder of the cop that Dinero had mistakenly killed the year before. Keece couldn't just sit back and let him ruin their organization with his bad decisions. He hoped that Dinero had learned from his mistakes and wouldn't take it to heart when he heard the news.

"Yeah, you're right. He fucked up big time, but I know he's going to be hurt. He's the sensitive one," Big joked.

"He'll get over it."

"Here comes her stupid ass now," Big said, alerting Keece that Danica was out.

Danica walked over to the truck and got in the back seat. She was a pretty girl, standing at 5'4 with short hair and mocha skin.

"Thanks for bailing me out, bro. Hey, Keece!" she sang happy to be out.

"Thanks my ass! I'm not bailing your fool ass out no more. You gon' sit in that bitch next time," Big threatened her.

"Yeah, you said that last time. You know you love me," she teased.

For the remainder of the ride, Big and Danica went back and forth while Keece laughed at their antics. Although Big played tough, he always had a soft spot for his little sister. Sometimes Keece wished that he had a sister to look after. He figured it would be easier than looking out for his hard-headed brothers all the time.

CHAPTER NINE

Paris opened her eyes and was met with pitch black darkness. She tried to sit up but was greeted with a migraine headache so painful that it hurt her to blink. Paris rubbed her temples, attempting to soothe the throbbing sensation inside of her head. She quickly remembered being in a scuffle with Chase and hopped up from what she guessed was a bed. Paris looked for a window or a door, but it was hard because she couldn't see a thing. After feeling for something that could lead her out of the room, she found the window. She hurried and tried to lift it but found it almost impossible. After the failed attempt with the window, Paris then walked over and found the door knob. She tried desperately to open the door but to no avail.

Minutes later, the door swung open, and Paris was knocked flat on her butt. The lights suddenly came on, and she was greeted by Chase. Paris winced at the bright lights that were causing her headache to become worse.

"You finally up, huh?" Chase asked with a crooked grin.

"Fuck you! Let me out of here, Chase," Paris snapped at him, scooting to the opposite side of the room.

"I already told you I can't do that. The deal is done, P," he replied sitting on the bed.

Paris stood up and wrapped her arms around her body. "You know human trafficking is illegal, right? Why would you do this to me, Chase? I thought you cared about me," she cried.

Chase sighed, feeling guilty about the position he'd put her in. His cousin had introduced him to the sex trafficking business almost a year ago. When his cousin first presented the idea to Chase to join him in the business, he vehemently declined. But when he revealed to Chase how much money he'd made from selling women, Chase decided to give it a try.

"I do care about you, Paris, but this opportunity fell into my lap. Out of all of the girls I've sold, I feel bad doing it to you. But like I said before, I gotta get this money," he spoke apologetically.

Paris began to pace back and forth frantically. She was shocked that Chase had revealed that he'd sold girls before. Paris wanted no part of his operation, so she came up with a plan.

"Okay, I'll give you the money if you need it that bad. How much is he paying you again?" she asked, hoping he would change his mind.

Chase gave her a curious look. "Twenty G's. Your ass ain't got it, so stop playing with me."

"I do have it. Hello? I'm an *attorney*. I have that in my savings account," she lied.

Chase looked at her intently while contemplating her offer. The truth was that Paris didn't have twenty thousand dollars. She really had about nine thousand tucked away into her savings. She knew that she was possibly playing with fire, but she was willing to do anything so she wouldn't be sold into human trafficking.

"A'ight, I'll take you up on your offer, but I'm not calling the guy to call it off until I have the money in my hand. If you're playing me, I swear I'm going to kill your ass," he threatened.

Paris smiled on the inside with pleading eyes. "I promise I'm not playing you. All we have to do is go to the bank tomorrow and you'll have your money," she said all in one breath. She silently prayed to God for it to be her way out.

Chase nodded his head. "Okay, we'll go tomorrow. In the meantime, come over here." he demanded.

Paris' heart dropped when he gave her a lustful glare.

"For what?" she asked worriedly.

Chase narrowed his eyes. "Just do what I said! Now get the fuck over here!"

Paris trembled as she walked slowly over to Chase. She stood in front of him as his lustful eyes traveled up and down her body.

Please, God, don't let him rape me, she said to herself.

"Lay down," he spoke intensely.

Tears began to stream down her face as she thought about what would be happening next. "Please, Chase, you don't have to do this," Paris cried as he stood.

"Don't make me get aggressive with you again, Paris. Just let this shit flow," he said, guiding her backward on the bed.

Paris wept softly as she fell onto the bed. Chase went straight to Paris' neck and began licking and biting her roughly. She cringed as Chase pinched her nipples. Tired of the foreplay, Chase pushed her maxi skirt up and pulled her panties to the side. After releasing his dick, he plunged himself deep into her vagina, causing Paris to scream out in pain. She was nowhere near lubricated as Chase stroked fast and hard into her sex.

"Come on, Paris, baby. You gotta relax and get wet for me," he panted in her ear as her body tensed up.

Paris continued to cry, hoping he would climax soon. She never thought she would've been in a position to be raped. At that very moment, images of her mother, Camara, and even Keece popped into her head as Chase grunted and released himself inside of her. He lay on top of her for a minute before he got up and zipped his pants. Paris was thankful for the painful moment to be done and over with.

He wiped beads of sweat from his forehead. "I'm going to bed. I'll see you in the morning," he said, closing the door and locking it.

Paris rolled over and stared into the darkness, hoping that her plan would be her way to escape from this nightmare.

****

Dom sat inside of his car second guessing what he was about to do. It was way overdue for him to right his wrongs, and he honestly felt it was his only option. After he was released from the hospital months ago, Dom thought his sons would be right by his side, ready and willing to repair their broken relationship, but his plan had actually backfired. Keece and Dinero would call every blue moon, while Kiyan had chosen not to stay in contact with Dom at all. It hurt his feelings tremendously, but he didn't know what to do. He figured his only option was to finally apologize to Rochelle and profess how sorry he was.

Dom had truly loved Rochelle, and even to this day, he held special feelings for her. When he found out about her *alleged* affair, he lost his mind. He had given her everything, but she had supposedly turned around and stabbed him in the back with his best friend. Now that the truth had finally come out, Dom felt like a fool. He also felt like he had cheated himself and his sons out of a life with Rochelle. Dom regretted his decision to ever listen to Celine and take Rochelle away from their children.

He stood in front of Kiyan's home and rang the doorbell. His stomach was filled with knots and butterflies as he anticipated Rochelle's reaction. Minutes later, Rochelle answered the door with baby Milan in her arms. Instantly, her face formed a mean scowl, and she sucked her teeth. To Dom, she still was one of the most beautiful women he'd ever encountered.

"What are you doing here?" she asked in a snidely manner.

Dom tucked his hands into his pockets. "Actually, I'm here to talk to *you*, Rochelle, and to see *her*," he said, referring to Milan.

Rochelle rolled her eyes and gave him a screw face. "Dom, I don't wanna talk to your bitch ass, but you're welcome to come in and see your granddaughter," she snapped, allowing him to come inside.

Dom grabbed the baby from Rochelle, and she walked off toward the kitchen to separate herself from Dom. She found herself scratching every time she was in his presence. Dom took a gamble, and decided to follow Rochelle to the kitchen where he found her sitting at the island cutting up onions.

"So where is Kiyan?" he asked, bouncing the baby in his arms.

"Running the streets," she replied with an attitude.

Dom took a seat next to her. "So why won't you talk to me, Chelle?"

Rochelle dropped the knife and looked him dead in the eyes. "My name is *Rochelle* to you, and we don't have shit to talk about, Dom," she snapped.

Dom cleared his throat. He looked briefly at Milan, who was slobbering all over his fingers.

"Actually, I want to apologize to you. I was wrong. I was *so* wrong in the way that I handled you, and I feel like shit because of it," Dom spoke apologetically. "I should've never taken the boys away from you because you didn't deserve that, and neither did they. I hate that I hurt you and took Celine's word over yours. Rochelle, I'm truly sorry."

Rochelle sucked her teeth, totally unmoved by his late apology. "Dom, your apology don't mean shit to me, okay? You come in here over twenty years later, and you think I'm supposed to forgive you for taking the kids that I gave birth to out of my life? You got me fucked up if you think it was going to be that easy! You had me beaten up, shot at, and arrested. Did you forget all of that shit? I missed my sons' first days of school, parent-teacher conferences, and when their first teeth fell out. I missed all of that shit, and you think your apology is going to fix it! Hell no, it ain't! So you and your apology can go to hell!"

Dom's shoulders sank. "I get it."

"No, you don't! You didn't have to live without your kids, so don't act like you understand my feelings because you never will! Let me ask you this; if I would've never popped up, would you have ever told them the truth?"

Dom sat silently for a moment, contemplating her question. He honestly didn't know if he would've had the courage to tell his sons the truth. "I honestly don't know, Rochelle," he said being truthful.

Rochelle scoffed. "Yeah, I figured that. You and your bitch would've gone along like y'all were the fucking

84

Huxtable family, all the while painting a bad picture of me. Oh, and if you would've told me your plan beforehand, I would've informed you that this shit would backfire on your dumb ass. Now look at you. Your sons don't even respect you anymore. Then you tried to kill yourself, thinking that shit would help your situation when in actuality, you look like a clown. I know you, so I know for a fact that you weren't really trying to kill yourself. You were being selfish as usual, trying to bait the boys back into your corner," she snapped, calling him out.

Dom sat quietly trying to keep his anger inside. Every word Rochelle had spoken to him stung him like a killer bee. She was right about everything, and he hated that. No one had ever talked to him in that manner, but he knew he deserved every bit of what Rochelle had said.

Dom stood. "You know what? I'm going to go," he declared and handed the baby over to Rochelle.

She took the baby and sat her inside of her bouncer. Dom walked out with tears on the brims of his eyes. His sons hated him, Rochelle hated him, and his wife would soon become his *ex-wife*. His life was in so much turmoil, and he didn't know how to fix it.

He did the one thing he hadn't done in years, and that was pray to God.

CHAPTER TEN

Chase walked into the bedroom where Paris was sleeping and shook her softly. She stirred a bit before finally opening her eyes. She had dreamed that she was at home in her bed, but was quickly disappointed when she saw that Chase was standing over her. Paris sat up slowly still a little sore from the night before.

"Here, use this to clean up so we can go to the bank." He handed her a bar of soap, a towel, and a toothbrush.

Paris grabbed the things from his hand and watched him walk out of the room. Since there was a bathroom connected to the bedroom, Paris slowly walked over and began to take care of her hygiene. She looked in the mirror and noticed that her eye was swollen shut due to the punch Chase had delivered the night before.

I look fucking terrible, she cried to herself.

After washing up, Paris got on her knees and prayed that God would make a way for her to escape Chase. When she was done, she walked out of the bathroom and was startled when she saw Chase sitting on the bed.

"Look, don't try no funny shit when we go to this bank. We're going to go in to get the money, and then I'll drive you home. I'll be sure to make the call to the guy who was coming to pick you up. After that, you'll never have to see me again," Chase said with no emotion.

Truthfully, Chase had no intention of letting Paris go. Ever since she had presented him with the idea that she would give him the money, he figured he would get double and still sell her. He knew it was wrong to get her hopes up, but he couldn't pass up the opportunity to make forty thousand instead of twenty thousand dollars.

"You promise to let me go after I give you the money?" Paris asked, still unsure if he was telling the truth.

He looked at her and lied to her face. "Yeah, I promise. Now let's go."

Paris followed him out of the room and downstairs. She walked toward the TV room but was stopped by Chase.

"What are you doing?" he asked, walking up on her.

"I just wanna get my phone," she replied.

Chase snorted. "Don't even try it. You're not getting that phone, but I do have your purse right here on the table. Now bring your ass on before I change my mind."

Paris discreetly rolled her eyes and grabbed her purse from the entryway table. She then followed Chase outside to his car. She couldn't believe how naïve she'd been in dealing with Chase. Paris had never picked up on his psychopathic behavior. She wanted to kick herself for not paying better attention.

"Which bank?" he asked, starting the engine.

"You can go to the U.S. Bank on 52nd and North Avenue," she replied softly.

Chase nodded his head and then started driving. When he stopped at the stoplight, Paris got the urge to open the door and make a run for it. Her palms became sweaty and her heart rate began to skyrocket, as she toyed with the idea.

I should make a run for it, she thought.

"Don't even try it, P. I got the child proof locks on." He smirked.

Shit! Was I that fucking obvious? Paris asked herself.

After twenty minutes of riding in anxiety filled silence, they finally arrived at the bank. Chase turned and looked at Paris, who was purposely looking forward. All kinds of thoughts were going through her mind as she tried to devise the right plan to escape.

"Aye, make this shit quick, a'ight? In and out. I don't wanna have to fuck you up. Now put these glasses on," he threatened as he threw the glasses in her lap.

Paris picked up the sunglasses and slid them on her face. Chase threw a baseball cap on with some oversized sunglasses. After making sure that his eyes were concealed, he put his hood on his head that hid most of his face. Chase got out of the car and walked around the car to open her door. She got out and walked behind Chase, who then grabbed her hand. Just the feel of his skin on hers almost caused Paris to vomit.

When they walked inside, Paris went to the kiosk table to fill out a withdrawal slip, while Chase stood next to her making sure he kept his eyes on her.

Paris nervously grabbed the pen and began to write her name. Her hand was trembling so bad that even she couldn't recognize her own handwriting.

How can I get out of this?

Instantly, an idea popped in her head, but before executing it, she looked up at Chase first. He was scrolling through his phone, not paying attention to her at the moment. Taking that as her cue, Paris began to write a note at the bottom of the slip.

"Hurry up." he said, startling her.

Paris hurried and covered the note with her ID so Chase wouldn't see it. Since she had been a regular customer for a certain period of time, some of the employees gave her head nods and even hand waves. She stood in the line for the teller, who she often would talk to more than the others. Chase was standing so close to her that she could feel his hot breath flowing across her neck.

Paris slowly stepped up to the counter.

"How are you, Ms. Parker?" the teller asked.

She was a young college student who had a great personality. She and Paris would converse every time she came in.

Paris smiled. "I'm good. How about you?" she asked, putting on her game face.

Chase stood closely beside her while looking at the teller.

"I'm fine. Just happy it's the weekend," she smiled sweetly.

The bank teller grabbed the slip and began to type in Paris' information, but stopped when she noticed the note at the bottom, which read *"Pls help me."*

The teller looked up into Paris' face who gave her a desperate look with pleading eyes. Usually, whenever Paris visited the bank, she was chipper and happy. The teller could now further sense that something wasn't right because Paris usually came alone. The teller then briefly looked at Chase who had his back turned.

"Ms. Parker, because this is such a large withdrawal, I'm going to have to take you to the back where I can take your fingerprints and give you the money in a complimentary bag," she said, playing it off.

Paris silently breathed a sigh of relief and started walking toward the back with Chase latched to her heels.

The teller noticed that he was walking to the back with Paris, and she stopped him. "I'm sorry, sir, but only account holders are allowed to go to the back."

Paris held her breath as she awaited Chase's response. She prayed that he would take the bait and not make a big deal about it.

Chase looked back and forth between the teller and Paris. "Okay, I'll wait out here," he replied, giving Paris a look that said, "Don't try it." He then stepped close to her and bent down. "Don't fuck with me, Paris. Hurry up," he whispered in her ear.

Paris nodded, followed the teller and waited for her to shut the door.

"Girl, what the fuck? What's going on with you and that guy?" the teller asked.

Paris began to pace the floor frantically. "Oh, my God, you have to get me out of here! He's trying to kidnap me!" she pleaded.

The girl gasped. "Do you want me to call the police?"

Paris rapidly nodded her head. "Yes, please. He needs to be arrested. He's trying to sell me to another man. Please go and call them," Paris begged her.

The teller grabbed Paris' shoulders to calm her down. "Okay, I'll go and call them. Did he hurt you?" she asked her.

Paris snatched off the sunglasses, revealing her swollen eye. The teller winced as she looked at Paris' face.

"Look at what he did to my eye. You have to help me escape. I can't go back out there," Paris pleaded.

"Okay, okay...look, just stay back here, and I'll explain everything to my manager. I'm going to go and call the police and alert our guard of the situation so he won't let him run. Just sit tight. I promise we'll get you out of here.

The teller walked Paris to the conference room as she took a seat. The teller then closed the door and walked back to the front. Paris breathed a sigh of relief as she tried to steady her breathing. Her heart was still beating a mile a minute, but Paris wasn't concerned about that. She was grateful that God had answered her prayers and allowed her to escape the horrors of Chase.

Paris sat back anxiously and waited for the police.

****

Chase sat inside of the lobby at the bank with nervousness running through his body. It had now been passed five minutes, and Paris wasn't back yet. He looked at his phone and then at the door, hoping she would be out at any minute. His leg shook vigorously as his chest tightened.

Seconds later, the bank teller came back to the front without Paris behind her. She stopped to talk with the security guard briefly before he looked over at Chase. Chase stood up frantically and attempted to make a beeline to the door. He could tell by the looks on their faces that Paris had alerted her of his plan. The security guard hurried and tried to grab Chase before he could walk out. Chase yanked his arm out of the guard's grasp and then tried to run. The guard quickly caught up to Chase and grabbed his collar, yanking him back towards him. Chase's hood fell backward while his sunglasses sat crooked on his face. Upset that the guard was trying to reprimand him, Chase hit the guard with a right hook, instantly dropping him to the floor. A male customer tried to help the guard but tripped over his own foot and fell, just as he was running toward him. Chase took his chance and ran out of the bank with his head down.

Patrons ran over to the guard to help him to his feet while he held his eye.

"Please go get that man's license plate number!" the guard yelled to no one in particular.

A woman ran out and looked around the parking lot in search of Chase. When she couldn't spot him, she walked further into the lot. When she saw a black Challenger speed out of the exit, she ran towards the street he was traveling on but was unable to get the license plate's number, so she ran back into the bank.

"I'm sorry, but he was going so fast that I couldn't get a number," she spoke apologetically.

The guard huffed. "It's fine. Did you at least see what type of car he was driving?"

"Yes, it was a black Challenger with black rims."

The teller walked back over to the guard and the woman. She had just gotten off the phone with the police. "Thank you. I'll let the police know when they come. They should be on the way," she said

"Where is the victim?" the guard asked.

"She's in the back."

"Well, at least she's safe. Hopefully the surveillance video will help ID this guy."

CHAPTER ELEVEN

Camara sat at her desk calling Paris for the third time that morning. Each time she called, she would reach her voicemail. She and Paris usually talked every morning on their way to work. The fact that she hadn't called made Camara skeptical. She finally decided to call her office to see if maybe she was busy and that's why she couldn't talk.

"Law offices of Paris Parker. How can I help you?" Aimee answered.

"Hey, Aimee, it's Camara. Is Paris available?"

"No. Actually she didn't come in yet, which is weird. I had to reschedule one of her clients who'd been here waiting in the office."

Instantly, Camara's heart dropped. "What?" she quipped. It was unlike Paris to keep a client waiting. Suddenly, she became worried.

"Okay, I'll try to find her," Camara said and hung up.

The last time Camara remembered speaking to Paris was before her date with Chase. She kicked herself for not getting more information on him. She knew he was a mechanic, but she didn't know which auto shop he worked at. Camara grabbed her phone and started dialing Paris' mother's number, but her call was interrupted by a private number. Thinking that it may be Paris, she answered.

"Hello?"

"Camara, I need you to come and get me," Paris spoke in a panicky tone.

Camara stood up from her desk in a panic. "Where the hell have you been? Everyone has been looking for you," she fussed.

"I'm at the police station. Some things happened with Chase that I'll tell you about when you get here. I don't want to explain it over the phone."

"Oh my God, Paris! Okay, which police station should I come to?"

"Come to the one on Lisbon Avenue. Across from Judy's."

"All right, I'm on my way," she said and then hung up.

Camara hurried and grabbed her keys. She told her boss that she had a family emergency, left out of the building and hurried to her car. Camara was so shocked by Paris' little revelation that she could hardly get her key in the ignition. After starting up the car, Camara made her way to the police station, breaking every speed limit known to man. All she could think about was getting to Paris and making sure she was safe.

After a fifteen minute drive, Camara turned down the street and pulled into the police station parking lot. Camara jumped out of the car and then ran inside of the building. She walked up to the front desk where she was greeted by a female officer. Camara began to explain why she was there until she saw Paris seated in the office toward the back. Camara pointed her out to the officer where she led Camara back to where Paris was.

Camara ran up to her and hugged her. "What the fuck happened?" she asked.

Paris shook her head, feeling defeated and tired. "That bitch, Chase, tried to kidnap me and sell me into that human trafficking shit! I've been held hostage since last night. You wouldn't believe what I went through," she said in a low tone.

"Did he hurt you, Paris?" Camara asked, taking a seat next to her.

Paris took off her sunglasses to show Camara her swollen eye. Immediately, Camara covered her mouth with her hand. It hurt Camara tremendously to see that Paris was in pain.

"What the fuck? I'm about to call the fucking crew to whoop his ass!" Camara snapped, grabbing her phone.

Paris took the phone out of her hand. "Not right now. I just filed a report with the police and gave them all of the information that I had on Chase. I need to go to the hospital because he... raped me last night." Paris could feel the tears gather in her eyes as she thought about Chase sexually assaulting her.

Tears formed in Camara's eyes. "Aw, Paris, come here."

Camara grabbed Paris and then held her tightly. Paris sobbed in her arms, causing Camara to cry along with her. She felt bad because she hadn't been there to help or protect Paris.

"Okay, let's go to the hospital. Are you done here?"

"Wait a second. I'm just waiting on the officer to finish up his report," Paris informed her.

After the police got the necessary information from Paris, he assured her that they would follow up with the bank. They were hopeful that the surveillance video would identify Chase. The officer gave Paris his contact information and finally released her.

Camara drove to Froedtert Hospital where they checked Paris in. Camara made sure to call her mother so she could meet them there. She was so consumed with anger that her heart began to pound violently inside of her chest. Camara wanted to track Chase down and kill him herself. She had already made up her mind to call Kiyan so he could get more information on him.

After the doctor did his physical exam and thorough STD check, Camara was allowed to go back in the room with Paris.

"How do you feel?" Camara asked Paris, rubbing her back.

Paris shrugged her shoulders and took a sip of her water. She just wanted the nightmare to be over and done with. Deep down she knew life for her would never be the same. Her outlook on men and the dating scene had been tainted. She felt dirty by the rape and wondered if she would ever recover.

Minutes later, Paris' mother, Shonda, rushed in, "Oh, my baby! Are you okay?" she asked, hugging Paris.

Without thinking, Paris broke down in her mother's arms. That maternal comfort soothed her soul as she wept in her mother's arms. She had never wanted to hurt her mother like this, and even though it wasn't her fault, it still pained her that her mother had also been affected.

"Listen, we are going to get through this. Do you have any information on this guy? Shit, I'm ready to go look for his ass myself!" her mother snapped.

"I told the police everything that I knew. All I know is his name, birthday, and the name of the auto shop where he works. I do remember where the house was located. I'm sure he probably changed his number by now. Camara, please look on his Facebook page for me and try to screenshot some pictures of him," Paris said, feeling overwhelmed.

Camara pulled out her cell phone and immediately looked for Chase's page. After minutes of trying to locate the page, she gave up without any success.

Camara gave her a frustrated look. "Why can't I find it? I bet his sheisty ass deleted it."

Shonda shook her head. "What's that other shit y'all use sometimes with the pictures?"

"Instagram?" Paris quizzed.

"Yeah. That's it. Does he have one of those?"

Paris shook her head. "Nah. I only knew about his Facebook page," she said softly.

"Didn't he pick you up from your house? That means he knows where you live, Paris. You shouldn't go back there," Camara told her.

Paris sighed and covered her eyes. She didn't even want to think about the possibility of Chase coming back for her at her home. "I know. I need to duck off some place where he wouldn't know to come. Ma, I wouldn't feel safe at your house. Who knows how much he knows about you and me."

"You can come stay with Kiyan and me. We have more than enough room," Camara offered.

Paris gave her a weak smile and shook her head. "I appreciate the offer, but I don't want to intrude on you and your little family. Plus, I know that Kiyan's mom is staying there."

Camara waved her hand. "Girl, you won't be intruding. Kiyan would understand. Trust me," she insisted.

"Actually, I want to be alone. I hate that I have to take time off of work, like I can really afford that. But I can't work like this," Paris spoke with tears flowing from her eyes.

Shonda got up from her chair and hugged Paris tightly. "Honey, you don't need to be alone right now. Just come back home," she begged.

"Look, Kiyan owns a lot of condos around the city. Maybe you can stay at one of them until this guy is caught."

Paris wiped her eyes. "You think Kiyan would be okay with that?"

"Yeah. I'll call him right now."

Paris was so grateful for Camara and her eagerness to help. Paris didn't know what she would do without her. Paris couldn't imagine going back to her home while Chase was still on the loose. She hoped like hell that the police would find him because she couldn't see herself living a peaceful life with him still on the streets.

CHAPTER TWELVE

"Why you trying to leave, bro?" Kiyan asked Keece as they sat in the conference room at their construction office. Big had just informed Kiyan and Dinero about Keece's plan to leave their drug business.

Keece shrugged. "I just feel like it's time for me to chill," he responded.

"What? Man, you trippin'," Dinero said, waving Keece off.

Kiyan sat up and rested his forearms on the table. "You can't do that, Keece. We said we would be in this shit together. You can't just change our oath like that," he argued.

Big nodded. "That's what I said too."

Keece chuckled because they were actually trying to gang up on him over his decision. He knew they would never understand because they lived for that type of life.

"This shit ain't fun no more to me. What do y'all want me to do?" Keece asked.

"That's because shit has been running smoothly. What you need is some action. You want us to start a war?" Dinero joked with a grin on his face.

Keece waved his hand at Dinero. "Fuck outta here," he said with a chuckle.

"Listen, you can't just leave this shit. We need you here to run things. If it wasn't for you, we wouldn't be making as much money as we do," Kiyan told him.

Keece laughed. "Man, go on. You and Big can handle it. Don't try to sweet talk me, bro," he told Kiyan.

Dinero instantly twisted his face when Keece didn't mention his name. He couldn't understand why Keece thought he wouldn't be able to run their business.

"You don't think *I* would be able to handle it?" Dinero asked.

Big shuffled in his seat because he knew Dinero would be offended by not being included.

Keece paused briefly before speaking. "I think you could, but not right now."

Dinero sucked his teeth and sat back in his chair. "You're still not over that shit with Dyno? Damn, how long ago was that?"

"Nigga, it ain't been long enough! Just because it brought us closer to Mama, it doesn't mean you didn't fuck up," Keece snapped, matching Dinero's attitude.

"That's fucked up. So you were gon' put them in charge and just leave me here to be an errand boy or some shit?" Dinero countered.

Keece shot him the most vicious look ever. "Are you an errand boy now? Aye, for real, you better leave me the fuck alone before you piss me off. I never saw a mothafucka fuck up and want a reward after it. You think Pops would've promoted you? Hell no, he wouldn't have. You would've been working the front desk at the office."

Dinero stood. "Man, fuck this. I'm out!" he snapped and left.

Keece had expected that response from Dinero. It was how he acted whenever he didn't get his way. He never wanted to be held accountable for his actions, and he always thought his mistakes should be overlooked. Keece wouldn't be able to trust Dinero with their family operation until he showed that he could make good business decisions.

Kiyan chuckled. "Damn, bro is hot with you. You know you gotta talk differently with his sensitive ass."

Big laughed. "I told him."

Keece sucked his teeth. "Man, fuck that. He a grown-ass man, and I'm not about to baby his ass so his feelings won't be hurt. I don't do it for nobody else, and I'm not about to start with him."

Kiyan's phone rang, and he noticed that it was Camara.

"This is Camara. I'll be right back," Kiyan said and stepped outside.

Big and Keece started talking about Dinero and other subjects. After ten minutes, Kiyan returned with a weird look on his face.

"What's wrong?" Keece asked.

"That was Camara asking me to put Paris up in one of my buildings. She said something happened to her."

Keece's heart began to race as visions of Paris being hurt flashed through his mind. No, they were no longer a couple, but Keece still loved and cared for her deeply.

"Something like what?" Keece instantly grilled him.

Kiyan shrugged. "She didn't tell me. It must be something bad because she said that they were leaving the hospital. She wants me to meet her at the condo."

Suddenly, Keece became upset that Paris was actually in the hospital. "She was in the *hospital*? What the fuck?"

He pulled out his cell phone and then dialed Paris' number. Although they weren't together anymore, he still didn't want to see any harm come to her. When her phone went to voicemail, he hung up.

"Did she answer?" Big asked.

Keece shook his head and stood up from his seat. "Nah. Aye, Kiyan, I'ma ride with you to meet them."

"A'ight, let's go."

****

Camara, Paris, and Shonda pulled up to the condo where Paris would be staying. After talking with the doctor and nurses for what seemed like hours, she was beyond exhausted. All she wanted to do was take a sleeping pill and drift off from her reality. Although she had told Camara that she wanted to be alone, Paris had begun to have second thoughts as the night time approached. She was terrified of the nightmares that she knew were waiting for her.

"There's Kiyan now," Camara announced.

They all got out of the car and walked over to Kiyan's car. Paris was surprised when she saw Keece get out on the passenger's side and walk over to her.

Shit! I'm not prepared for this, Paris ranted to herself.

Keece grabbed her face and examined her swollen eye. "Who hurt you?" he demanded.

"This guy..." she said in a low tone.

Keece clenched his jaw. "What's his name?"

"Chase... Keece, don't worry about it. The police will look for him," she tried to assure him.

Keece walked away and wiped his hands over his face. Seeing her in pain caused him to fume inside. "I ain't trying to hear that! What else did he do?" he barked.

"Keece, let's go in the house so y'all can talk in private," Camara suggested.

Keece looked at Camara for a moment and nodded his head. They all gathered inside the condo and looked around. Keece was livid, and he wanted Paris to tell him the whole story. Seeing her eye swollen made him want to tear up the city. If she had been sexually violated, there was no telling what he was capable of doing. He still felt like Paris belonged to him, even though they were separated. He would still kill anyone who caused her any pain.

"Come here, Paris," Keece demanded from his position inside the kitchen.

Paris walked into the kitchen and stood face to face with Keece. When he looked at her, it almost made her cry. She felt so dirty and exposed. She could tell that Keece already knew what had really happened in that house.

"You don't need to be staying here by yourself, especially with that nigga on the run."

Paris released a sigh. "I'm not about to go back to my house. He knows where I live."

"You should just come back to my crib until this shit is over, and I ain't taking no for an answer," Keece told her, referring to his home that they used to share.

Paris raised her brow. "Keece, I'm not about to go back there, especially since you got you a new bitch," Paris protested.

Keece gave her a dirty look. "That's really on your mind right now? I'm trying to make sure that you're safe and protected, and you're standing here talking about another bitch?"

"You know what? I'm not about to get into this right now. I don't think going to your house would be a good idea like I said."

Keece sucked his teeth. "So what are you about to do? You gon' sit here by yourself? You don't know if he followed you from the hospital or not. You really trying to take that chance?"

"Does it look like I'm trying to take that chance, Keece?" she snapped. "And stop yelling at me. I have a damn headache."

Shonda came into the kitchen after she'd heard the commotion between the two.

"What's going on?" Shonda asked, standing next to Paris.

"Keece doesn't think I should stay here. He offered to let me stay at his home, but I don't know if that's the best thing to do." Paris spoke while rubbing her temples. She just wanted this day to be over.

Shonda exhaled. "I mean, I would stay here with you if you needed me to, but maybe you should consider his offer. At least you'll be safer with a man to protect you."

Paris looked at her mother and thought about what she had just said. No, she didn't want to stay by herself, but then again, she was skeptical about going back to Keece's home as well. She didn't want to feel awkward and uncomfortable around him. However, Paris could tell by the look on his face that she had no other choice.

"But don't you have a girlfriend? How will she feel about me staying with you?" Paris wanted to know.

"*Damn*, Paris, don't worry about all of that! Plus, I don't have a girlfriend," Keece snapped and walked off into the living room where everyone else was.

"She's not going to stay here. I'm taking her back to my house where I know she'll be safe. Ms. Shonda, you're welcome to stay there too if you want," he offered.

"Thank you, Keece," Shonda said.

They all left out of the condo and hopped inside of their cars. Since Keece lived close to Kiyan, Paris decided to ride back with Camara. She was secretly touched that Keece wanted to protect her. She would've thought that he didn't care by how their last encounter went, but nonetheless she was happy that he still cared about her well-being.

CHAPTER THIRTEEN

Case sat inside of Bar Louie located by Bayshore Mall, listening to his mother ramble about her divorce. He was tired of hearing about his parents' marital demise, and Celine didn't seem to get the hint. Case knew that he was the only person that his mother had in her corner, but he didn't want to be consumed by her drama. He had so many things going on in his life, and his mother had become a distraction.

"Sweetie, why aren't you eating your food? You feel okay?" she asked.

Case pushed his plate away, having lost his appetite. "Yeah, I'm good."

"So I was thinking about selling the house, if your father doesn't fight for it. I don't think I would be able to handle the bills on my own," she said sadly.

Case nodded, agreeing with her idea. "You don't really need that big of a house anyway."

"Yeah, I know. So what's going on with you? How's school?" she asked, taking a sip of soda.

Case knew what he was about to tell her would break her heart, but his mind had been set for a while.

"I'm not going back to school this fall," he blurted out.

Celine dropped her fork and gave Case a bewildered look. It had always been her dream for her child to go to college and earn a degree. Celine was adamant about Case not joining his brother's in their drug operation. She didn't want that for her child.

"What do you mean you're not going back? So you're just going to give up your scholarship?" she asked.

Case rolled his eyes and paused briefly. "Look, school isn't for me, and my love for football isn't there anymore. I tried to stick with it just to make you and dad proud, but it has made me unhappy, and I don't wanna do it anymore."

Celine rubbed her temples as she listened to Case crush her dream of him. "Case, baby, you cannot quit school. We made plans that you would either finish school or get drafted. You're such a talented football player. Do you wanna give that all up?" she asked with disappointment.

"Listen, Ma, I've made my decision already. I wasn't doing it for me, and it showed in my grades and on the field. You act like school is the only way to be successful."

"To me it is! You'll make it further in life when you have some sort of degree."

Case shook his head. "Not always. I know some people with master's degrees who are working with companies that have nothing to do with their field of degree. Plus, look at my brothers. They're successful, and they didn't go to college."

Celine spoke with so much hurt. "Yeah, but their success comes from *illegal* activities, and I don't want that for you. I've never wanted that for you."

Case shifted in his seat, not liking the way she was speaking about his brothers. "Ma, how're you gon' sit here and turn your nose up to their success when you were married to a man that came up off drug money? You had no problem with *illegal* activities when he was buying you mansions, cars, and jewelry. Don't be a hypocrite," he snapped.

Celine sat back in her seat, appalled that Case had spoken to her in that manner. He had never been disrespectful toward her, and she didn't like it one bit.

"Watch your mouth! Yeah, I was with a man who came up off drug money, but when I had you, I knew that I didn't want you to become a part of that world. When you have children, Case, your perspective changes. You won't understand until you have children of your own."

Case looked at his mother and then stared out of the window. He had known that she wouldn't agree with his decision, but he didn't care. The tension from the family drama had begun to stress him out to the point that it had started reflecting in his school work. Sleepless nights had caused him to miss practice and team meetings. He wasn't in the right frame of mind to be a college student.

Case laughed at his mother because she had always put him on a pedestal, labeling him as the good kid. The truth was that Case had done his share of dirt, but he was always able to hide it from Celine because his brothers used to constantly bail him out. It was because of him and his poor decision that had sent Keece to jail for a year. He didn't know the police would search the car that night and find his gun. After that incident, Case made a vow to himself that he would try and give college a chance, but it just wasn't for him.

"So what do you plan to do with your life, Case?" Celine asked, breaking him from his thoughts.

"Well, Keece is going to open up a tattoo shop, and he agreed to teach me how to tattoo. Who knows; this may be a start to a great career," he said, being optimistic.

Celine smacked her lips. "You want to be a tattoo artist?"

"You know what, Ma? I'm about to go. I'll talk to you later," Case said before he abruptly left out of the restaurant.

Celine had always been supportive of Case's decisions, but lately she had become a negative Nancy. Case chalked it up to her going through her own issues, but he was no longer going to stick around for her to tear him down.

****

"You know we all miss you down here, especially the girls."

Rochelle was on the phone with Carlos updating him on her new life in Milwaukee. Every week she and Carlos would talk and catch up on each other's lives. Rochelle couldn't lie. She missed the hell out of New Orleans, especially the food, but God had answered her prayers and reconnected her with her children.

"Aw, I miss you guys too. Tell them I'm coming to see them once my house is done."

Rochelle had recently purchased a house with the help of the boys, and it was now being renovated to her liking.

"Yeah, you know I had to check a couple people who thought that just because you were gone they didn't need to do their job," he said.

Rochelle used to run his bars when she was down in New Orleans. She missed the thrill of being in the company of the workers and patrons.

"You better. Shit, people would be quick to try and get over. Oh, I almost forgot to tell you that I had to whoop Celine's ass at the bar a couple weeks ago..."

"What? How did that ended up happening?" Carlos asked.

Rochelle filled Carlos in on the entire scene between her and Celine. He found it hysterical that it had taken them over twenty years to finally fight. He had known Celine for years and couldn't stand her jealous behavior. When he and Dom were still friends, Celine would throw herself all over him when Rochelle wasn't around. Carlos didn't understand how Dom didn't pick up on her scandalous behavior beforehand. Celine wasn't a person who could be trusted.

"She had that shit coming, though. My girl had to put the paws on her ass." He laughed.

"You're so silly," Rochelle said, joining him in laughter.

"Nah, but for real, I'm happy that everything came full circle for you. I always knew that you would get back to your boys, and I'm honestly happy for you, even though my partner in crime is gone."

Carlos words caused a lump to form in Rochelle's throat. He had been the only one in her corner when she had no one else. There were times when he could've turned his back on Rochelle, but he never did. She would always appreciate him for saving her from the dark moments when she'd felt like giving up. Carlos had talked Rochelle down from the ledge numerous times during their friendship. He had always offered his support no matter the situation.

Rochelle had a genuine love for Carlos. It wasn't in a sexual way. He was her dear friend, and she would give him her last because he had done it for her so many times before. He had always assured her that he would remain in her corner. Rochelle had never experienced a friendship so great, and she appreciated that Carlos had never tried to cross the friend zone.

"Aw, Carlos, you're going to make me cry. You know I'm not the emotional type," she said, tearing up.

"I'm not trying to make you cry. I'm just happy that you're finally in a good space, Chelle," he said genuinely.

"I am, but I do miss my life there. I promise I'll make it down there when I get situated here. I don't want you to think I've abandoned you guys," she assured him.

"I know you're not on that shit. Now tell me about the boys. What kind of men are they?"

CHAPTER FOURTEEN

Paris had been staying back at Keece's home for about a week now. Her mother had decided to stay with her since she was so worried about her mental health. Shonda was scared of what the effects of being raped would do to Paris, so she kept a close eye on her. Keece had offered to give her their former bedroom, but Paris opted to stay in one of the guest bedrooms. She didn't know if Keece had had sex with his new girlfriend in that bed or not, so she wanted no parts.

Keece had been in and out most of the time, so he could give Paris her space. When she was first attacked, Keece had wanted to know every detail, but now that he'd had time to cool off, he didn't want to know what had happened to her at that house. He knew that he wouldn't be able to handle the specific facts. Paris, on the other hand, was relieved that he hadn't asked her about the trauma that Chase had caused. She felt like if she were to reveal everything to

Keece, he would look at her differently even if he said he wouldn't.

Paris lay wide awake staring into the darkness like she had been doing for the past seven nights. Every time she tried to fall asleep, images of Chase raping her would invade her mind. She didn't know what kind of magic she needed to perform to get that man out of her head. She had tried praying him away, counting sheep, and even sleeping pills, but nothing seemed to help her psyche get rid of him.

Paris sat up in the bed and stood. She walked out of the guest room and headed down the hall to Keece's bedroom. She opened the door slowly and noticed that he wasn't in the bed. Walking further into the room, she saw that he was posted on the balcony. She opened the door and stuck her head out.

"Can I join you?" she asked softly.

Keece looked over his shoulder at her and nodded. He watched her walk from the door to sit on the side of him. For a moment, they sat in a comfortable silence while inhaling the night air. Paris missed the nights where they would sit out on the balcony and talk for what seemed like hours. She watched Keece sit with his tattoo-covered arms exposed while smoking a blunt. Being in his presence for the last couple of days had made her miss everything about him.

She had tried to fight it, but she couldn't help that her feelings for him were still present.

"You can't sleep?" he asked, pulling her from her thoughts.

"No. I'm super tired, though."

Keece glanced at Paris and then quickly looked away. He felt so bad for her and only wished that he could take her pain away. Now that she was in his presence, he was going to make sure that she was taken care of. No one would ever be able to hurt her again on his watch.

Keece sat back and sighed. "I don't wanna know how dude hurt you, but I do wanna know how you got away," he told her.

Paris sighed. "Well, he was going to sell me for twenty thousand dollars before I offered to pay myself. He agreed, so we went to the bank. I honestly didn't have a plan to get away, but I knew I was not about to walk out of that bank with him. So I wrote a note on the withdrawal slip and gave it to the teller. She read it and then helped separate Chase and I because he was all over me. She took me to the back and then she went to call the police. Keece, I was so scared. I just... I was so scared." She began to tear up because she still couldn't believe she had escaped that terrifying situation.

Keece scooted next to her and hugged her. He hated seeing Paris so broken and he couldn't do anything about it. He caressed her soft skin as he held her tight.

"You don't need to be scared anymore. I'm not going to let anything happen to you," he whispered to her.

Paris sniffled and continued to relish his presence. She felt so safe in Keece's arms and she believed him when he said that no one would hurt her again.

Paris reluctantly pulled back from his embrace. "I'm salty that he's still on the run."

"We've been looking for his ass, but we ain't been able to find him. We went to the address you gave us, but it was vacant," he informed her.

Paris exhaled slowly. "The police don't have any leads either. They reviewed the surveillance video from the bank and said that the quality was bad. I swear MPD ain't good for shit. They also informed me that all of the information I gave them was false. Nothing about Chase was the truth. He was playing me all along, and I feel so stupid for not checking into things like I normally would have. It's almost like I was asking for this shit," she spat, upset with herself.

She was the one who had insisted that they not take things too fast or become serious. She should've been more on guard.

"Don't say that. Nobody asks to be attacked and then sold into human trafficking. How long had y'all been talking?"

"Just for two months. It's crazy because I had finally let my guard down with him and allowed myself to go over to his house, which I found out later on was his cousin's home. Even that was probably a lie. I wish I would've never gone over there," she said sadly.

Keece didn't know what to say to comfort her. He hated that she felt like it was all her fault because it wasn't. Paris had just met the wrong man at the wrong time.

"Look at the bright side. At least you found a way to escape. How many girls can say that?" he offered.

Paris gave him a faint smile as she appreciated his encouraging words. "Yeah, you're right. I just want my life back, though. I need to go back to work to finish my cases. I've had to refer a lot of my clients to my colleagues because I'm unable to perform. Plus, I can't afford to take off from work."

"You don't need to go back to work right now, Paris. You gotta get yourself together."

Paris crossed her arms, trying to shield the cool breeze. "I know, but I feel like work would take my mind off this bullshit, and I feel bad because Aimee needs her job too."

"Don't worry about her. She's with Big, so I know she won't want or need for anything. He'll take care of her," Keece assured her.

Paris took in what Keece had said and agreed. She knew she wouldn't be on her usual A game if she went back to work so fast. But at the same time, she didn't want her career to suffer since she had been doing so well at work. Plus, having her own law office came with a hefty price.

"I kinda missed being here," Paris revealed.

Keece sat with a shocked look on his face. "Oh yeah?"

"Yeah, I miss sitting out here and listening to the crickets. It's peaceful out here."

Keece chuckled. "I can't tell you missed it, with the way that you stormed out that day you left. Your ass even took the leftover pizza."

Paris joined him in laughter. "I was hungry."

"I had my mouth ready for that shit too," he joked.

Paris rolled her playfully eyes. "Whatever. You showed your ass that day, so no, I was not leaving any food for you."

Silence fell upon them as they became lost in their thoughts. It was pleasant for Keece to see Paris laughing and smiling. He hated to see her walk around moping or staying locked in her room.

"You ever have any regrets?" Paris asked him.

"Nah, not really. Do you?"

"Yeah. I wish I would've taken my time before making the decision to end our relationship. I was mad and emotional at the time, but I should've cooled off first. I hate that I said those words to you because I could tell that it hurt your feelings, but I was so upset with you. When I found out that you had stayed out all night with Riley, I was livid, and then when you to lied to my face, it broke my heart. At that point, I didn't feel significant in your life, and that shit almost made me go crazy. As a woman, it hurts when your man is putting you in a position to feel as though there is competition. We began to feel threatened by that shit. I'm telling you this because I want you to understand why I told you I didn't love you enough. It was because I was hurt, Keece." Paris let a tear slip from her eye as she thought back on the demise of their relationship.

Keece felt like shit as he listened to Paris pour her heart out. He knew he had fucked up royally with her, but he didn't know it was to that extent. He had never wanted Paris to feel threatened by another woman, especially not Riley, because there was no competition between the two.

"I'm sorry I made you feel that way, but you need to know that I never spent the night with Riley. I was super drunk and fell asleep in my car. I know I made a bad decision by even going to Riley's house, and if I could take it all back, I would." He took his hand and placed it on the back of her neck and began to massage it gently.

Paris' heart began to play hop scotch inside of her chest as Keece's touch provided a calming sensation. Paris felt like she had opened up too much to Keece and she didn't like feeling vulnerable. She didn't mean to bring up their relationship but when she was in Keece's presence, her hidden feelings began to arise. Not liking the feeling she was experiencing, Paris stood up abruptly and looked down at Keece.

"I'm getting kinda of sleepy, so I'm going to lay down. I'll see you in the morning," she said and walked off.

Keece watched Paris leave, hoping that their discussion hadn't sent them ten steps backward. He knew it probably hurt Paris to talk about their break up but he wasn't the one who'd started the conversation.

Keece shrugged, continued smoking, and hoped what Chase did to her wouldn't be a burden on her for the rest of her life.

CHAPTER FIFTEEN

Dinero and Case browsed through Southridge Mall in search of the new Jordan's that had just come out. They were relatively close since they were the youngest of the DeMao bunch. Dinero was still hot with his other brother's because he felt left out of the business. Even though Kiyan and Big had nothing to do with it, he felt that they were in on the plan as well.

"Man, I thought you said your connect was gon' come through," Case said, walking next to Dinero.

"Man, that nigga got knocked a couple days ago. He can't even come through on some bail money," Dinero joked.

Case laughed. "That's fucked up. I bet these mothafuckas sold out, though."

"Nah. My lil homie put two pairs aside for me. I just gotta pay him an extra hundred, plus some free car washes," Dinero told him.

Both men walked into Champs in search of Dinero's Jordan connect. Once the connect saw Dinero, he instantly rushed to the back to retrieve the shoes. Dinero joined Case on the bench and scrolled through his phone.

"So you still not fucking with Keece after he said that shit to you?" Case asked him.

Dinero scoffed. "Man, right now fuck him. He acts like he ain't never fucked up before and that he's so fucking perfect. Then Kiyan and Big didn't even come to my defense. So that tells me that they feel the same way that Keece feels. Fuck them!" he ranted.

Case looked at him, not liking the way he was speaking about their brothers. "All you gotta do is redeem yourself and show them that you can handle business just like them. Shit, take on more responsibility if you need to, because you contributed to the success of the business too."

Dinero nodded. "Thanks, bro. I needed that for real.

Minutes later, they heard a familiar voice call out to them.

"Hey y'all," Riley sang, walking over to where they were seated.

Dinero mean mugged her as she stood there with her hands on her hips. He had never liked Riley, and he'd always been vocal about it. To him, she was nothing but a gold digger and a snake. He was happy that Keece had finally let her scandalous ass go.

"What's up, Riley?" Case greeted her.

Riley shifted her weight to one leg as she looked down at Dinero. "Dinero, you can't speak? I see you're still rude as fuck," she spat.

Dinero snorted, "You know I don't fuck with you like that. Don't come up in here acting brand new."

"*Anyway*, what are y'all doing here? Y'all trying to grab the new J's?" she asked, trying to open them up to ask about Keece.

Case simply nodded his head while Dinero looked the other way. There was no way he was going to hold a conversation with Riley.

"So how's your brother?" she asked timidly.

Dinero snickered. "Who *Kiyan*?" he joked, causing Case to laugh.

Riley smacked her lips, not amused by Dinero's antics. "No, smart ass. You know who I'm talking about. How is he doing, Case?"

"He's cool." Case smirked.

"Is he still with Paris?" she pried more.

"Nah...not anymore..."

Dinero tapped Case's arm. "Aye, don't tell this nosy bitch nothing else." Then he turned his attention to Riley, spitting, "Stay out of his fucking business. He don't want your shady ass no more, hoe."

"You know what? I wasn't talking to your punk ass. And call me another hoe," she countered.

"What is your soft ass gon' do, huh? You can't run to Keece 'cause he don't fuck with you no more," Dinero challenged, causing her to become more upset.

Riley rolled her neck as she talked, "Nigga, I'll call one of my cousins on your ass."

Dinero shot up and stood face to face with Riley. He didn't take to kind to threats and he wasn't about to let Riley think she could get a pass to do so.

"Bitch, if you ever threaten me again, I'll have your ass folded up in one of these dumpsters looking like you just walked off the set of The Walking Dead," he gritted through his teeth.

Case jumped up and stood between Riley and Dinero. He knew Dinero had no problem laying Riley on her ass, and he didn't want to see his brother go to jail.

"Aye, y'all, calm down. We're at a fucking mall," Case reminded them.

Riley and Dinero shared a couple more angry glances before Dinero returned to his seat. Seconds later, the

Champs' employee came from the back with their shoes. Dinero grabbed the boxes from him and walked to the register.

"Just tell Keece to call me," Riley told Case before she walked off.

Case shook his head, then chuckled. He didn't understand why Riley didn't take the hint and move on.

Dinero came back over with the shoes in the bag.

"Yo' crazy ass was really gon' drop her in the store?" Case asked, laughing.

"Hell yeah! I can't stand her funny-looking ass," Dinero said seriously.

"You're wild, bro. Let's go get something to eat. I'm hungry as fuck."

The pair traveled through the mall and ate at the food court. After leaving, Dinero dropped Case off at his car and then made his way to see Rochelle. He hadn't seen her in a couple weeks, and she was starting to throw shade. At first, he wasn't feeling Rochelle being around, but after learning the truth about her absence, he had actually welcomed her with open arms. It felt good to finally have a woman in his life who genuinely loved him. To him, nothing compared to a mother's love, and even though Celine had shown him love growing up, he knew that she hadn't loved him wholeheartedly, especially with her ill intentions.

Dinero pulled up to Kiyan's home since Rochelle was still staying there and hopped out.

I hope Kiyan's ass is not here, Dinero said to himself.

He rang the doorbell, and Rochelle answered seconds later.

"Can I help you?" Rochelle asked with a serious face.

Dinero smiled. "Come on, Mama, stop playing."

"Oh, so now you know who I am? Why I gotta call you to see if you're alive? You need to call and check up on your ol' lady more," she fussed while letting him in.

"My bad. I'll make more of an effort to check on you," he promised before he kissed her on the cheek. Dinero walked inside and followed her to the kitchen.

"Are you hungry? I'm making some smothered pork chops and potatoes."

"Nah, I just ate at the mall. Where is everybody at?" he asked.

"Well, your brother is running the streets as usual. Camara is working late, and the baby is down for her nap. What did you go to the mall for?" she asked while seasoning the meat.

Dinero took a seat at the table. "Some shoes."

Rochelle chuckled before speaking, "You know your father stopped over here the other day trying to apologize? I almost threw some boiling water on his smug ass. Then I had to slap the fuck outta Celine at the bar a while back. Bitch tried to get slick at the mouth like my hands ain't decent," Rochelle ranted.

Dinero choked on his water from laughing so hard. Rochelle was such an animated person whenever she told stories.

"Mama, you put the paws on her ass?" he asked, hyping her up.

"Hell yeah! That shit was long overdue. Talking about she and Dom are still together like I give a fuck. She's still trying to be in a competition with me when there is none."

Dinero scoffed. "She's definitely lying 'cause Case told us that they're getting a divorce."

"Good for them. Now what's on your mind? I can tell when something isn't right with my boy. Talk to Mama."

Dinero exhaled and debated on if he wanted to bring his mother into the mix between him and his brothers. He figured he had nothing to lose, so he told her about the argument that had gone down between him and Keece. Dinero knew that now that he had told his mother about

KEECE AND PARIS 2

their spat, she would keep it real. He figured that he may need some truth serum.

"Well, let me say this. If you were in another crew, they probably would've killed you for the stunt that you pulled. But because you're in business with your brothers, they gave you a break. You can't be mad at them because *you* ultimately made the mistake," Rochelle said, speaking in a tone that only a mother could. "I don't think Keece is punishing you, but he is being cautious since you've displayed that you make bad business deals. He just wants you to learn from your mistake, and when you argue with them and get defensive, it makes it seem like you didn't learn your lesson."

Dinero nodded his head and continued drinking his water. His mom was right about everything, and he knew that he had to get his act together before he did some serious damage.

"You're right, Ma... I'll eventually sit down and talk to them all," he assured her.

"You see, *communication* is the key to every relationship." She smiled.

Dinero smiled back, thinking about how blessed he was to have finally connected with his mother. Although he had fucked up and gotten played in the end, he honestly felt like it was a blessing in disguise. They would've never reconnected with their mother if it hadn't been for him. Dinero would never regret his mistake because he finally had his mother in his life and that was all he'd ever wanted.

****

One month later...

Keece walked into his house after spending the entire morning searching for a building for his tattoo shop. He'd seen a few good options, but nothing had drawn him into putting up an offer. He walked to the kitchen and grabbed a bottle of water from the fridge and made his way upstairs. He heard music coming from Paris' room, so he opened the door and poked his head inside. Paris was standing in the mirror combing her hair and singing along to Fabolous "Doin' It Well". Keece noticed that she was dressed in a black pencil skirt, fitted white T-shirt, and black kimono. He walked over to her iPod, then turned the music down.

"Where do you think you're going?" he asked her.

"I have to go meet a client today. He doesn't want anyone else working on his case."

Keece frowned instantly. "So what? Tell his ass to deal with it. It's only been like a month since your attack. I think it's too soon to be out."

Paris turned around slowly and walked over to him. She appreciated Keece so much, but she couldn't say no to this particular client because they had done extensive business together. Paris didn't want to burn a bridge with her client.

She rested her hand on Keece's shoulder, saying, "Don't worry. Aimee is coming with me, and we're going to meet him in a public place. I won't be gone that long, okay?"

"Where is your mom?" he asked

"I told her to go home. She's been here long enough."

Keece gave her an intense look. "I don't like you out by yourself. You gon' have to take my little .22 with you," he told her, walking to another bedroom.

Paris followed him, hoping he wasn't talking about a *gun*.

She smacked her lips. "Keece, I am *not* taking a gun with me."

"Well, you're not leaving out of this house then." Keece reached up into the closet and retrieved the little black pistol.

"Keece, I've never shot a gun. I'll probably pull a Plaxico."

"Look, just take the safety off and then pull the trigger. It's not that hard. You can do it."

Paris rolled her eyes and took the gun from his hand. She looked at it for a minute and then walked back to her room. She tucked the gun safely inside her purse before she put on her heels.

"Aye, when you get there call me, and call me after you leave too. You hear me, Paris?"

Paris huffed. "Yes, Keece, I hear you."

Paris got a text from Aimee telling her that she was outside. She grabbed her belongings and walked out of the room with Keece following her while giving her the same speech again and causing Paris to chuckle.

"Okay, Keece, I got it. Now bye," she said, opening the door.

Keece pulled her arm, ushering her closer to him. "Wait. Give Daddy a kiss before you go," he flirted.

She laughed. "Picture that."

"Okay...On the cheek then..."

Paris rolled her eyes playfully before she stood on her tippy toes to kiss his cheek. Keece turned his face just in time to catch her lips. He made sure to plant a nice wet kiss on her juicy lips.

Pissed that he'd played her, Paris pushed him. "Ugh! You get on my nerves. Bye!" she spat as she stormed off.

Keece continued laughing as he watched her get inside of the car with Aimee. Since he had no plans, he decided to go upstairs to his bedroom and watch a little ESPN before he met up with Big later.

As soon as he turned on the TV, he got a call from Alyssa on his cell. Instantly, a guilty feeling washed over his body because he had been so consumed with Paris that he had been putting Alyssa on the back burner.

"What's up, Alyssa?" he answered.

She smacked her lips. "Um, don't what's up me! Why haven't I heard from you? I miss you."

"I had a family emergency, but how much did you miss me, though?"

"If you come up to my job, I'll show you just how much," Alyssa purred.

"Bet. I'm on my way."

Keece hung up the phone and grabbed his keys before he left out of the house. He jumped in his Audi A7 and peeled off. He wasn't quite sure of what to do with Alyssa just yet. There was no doubt that he liked her a lot, but now that Paris was around him on a daily basis, the love that he'd tried to keep buried for her had resurfaced. Keece knew that Paris wasn't emotionally available or sound enough for a relationship, so he decided he would let things flow with Alyssa.

Alyssa was a nail technician at a spa located in Brookfield. Once Keece pulled into the parking lot, he sent

Alyssa a text message, telling her to come outside. He also sent a text to Paris to make sure that she was okay.

Minutes later, Alyssa strutted outside with a wide grin on her face. Her chocolate bronzed skin glowed under the sunlight while her jet black hair flowed through the wind.

"You don't fuck with me no more I see," she joked, getting inside the car.

Keece chuckled at her remark. "You know it ain't like that. Don't make me feel worse than I do."

"I'm just playing, boo, but I did miss you. *She* missed you too," Alyssa said rubbing her vaginal area.

Immediately, Keece's dick became rock hard. "Come over here," he instructed.

Keece reclined his seat back and watched as Alyssa's tiny frame climbed on top of him. Instantly, their mouths met and their tongues started a familiar dance. Keece was way past horny, so he skipped the foreplay and slid her skirt up to her waist. Alyssa unbuckled his belt and pulled his thick penis. Keece grabbed a condom out of the console and slipped it on.

Alyssa hurriedly slid down on his dick and she let a moan escape her lips. This was what she had been feigning for the last several weeks. Alyssa worked her hips and continued to bounce and roll on his dick. Keece grabbed her waist, making sure to control the pace since he wasn't ready to cum yet.

"Oh my...This feels so good, Keece," Alyssa cooed in his ear.

"Come on, baby, I need you to show me what this pussy do," Keece challenged her.

Alyssa then grabbed the back of Keece's seat and began to ride him for dear life.

****

Paris and Aimee had finally finished their meeting with their client and were walking back to the car. They had decided to meet at the Starbucks inside of Target. For the most part, Paris did well by not becoming a nervous wreck while out in public, but she'd still made sure to become aware of her surroundings. Paris had also kept her purse rested on her lap just in case she would have to use the little .22 Keece had given her.

"I don't see how you deal with that demanding ass client," Aimee complained, getting inside of the car.

Paris released a sigh. "Girl, I know, but he's real cool sometimes. He just likes his shit done right. That's all."

"I see, but you did really good for your first outing. How have you been coping?" Aimee inquired.

Paris buckled her seatbelt before she replied, "I've joined this forum for rape victims who've gone through similar experiences. It's been real therapeutic being able to talk with someone who has been through the same thing. I decided that I'm not going to let this mess hinder me. I don't want to be ducking and hiding for the rest of my life. So I had to give it to God and let Him deal with Chase. The police still haven't found him and neither did Keece. I think he may have skipped town, which is a good thing. Plus, you guys have been a huge help, especially Keece."

"That's because he still loves his boo thang," Aimee teased as she watched Paris' smile.

Paris rolled her eyes. "Shut up, girl. Nah, but for real, I think we'll always love each other. I don't see that going away ever," she revealed.

"Girl, y'all need to quit playing and get back together. Y'all know you guys won't be happy with other people."

Paris thought about what Aimee had just said. Before her attack, she was optimistic about moving on from Keece. Now that she was back in his presence and knew that Keece truly cared about her wellbeing, it caused a field of emotions to surface that she had tried to keep hidden.

"I don't know about that. I don't know if I'm even ready for a relationship right now.

Aimee gave her a sympathetic look before she returned her focus back to the road. "Just give it time, boo. You'll get back to your old self."

"Yeah, I'm sure," Paris said sarcastically.

"I'm just happy you're not suffering emotionally and mentally from everything. I've seen women who never recover after they've been raped. You're a strong woman, Paris. I admire that about you," Aimee spoke sincerely.

"Aww, that's sweet. Thank you," Paris said giving her quick hug while she was driving.

Paris looked at her phone and noticed that she'd missed a text from Keece. Paris dialed his number and listened as it rung.

****

Alyssa continued giving Keece the ride of his life. His phone rang. He glanced at the screen and noticed that it was Paris.

Fuck! he thought to himself.

Keece forgot that he had told her to call him when she was leaving her meeting. He didn't want to miss her call just in case she was in trouble, so he answered and gestured for Alyssa to be quiet.

"Hello?" he answered, trying to steady his breathing.

"Hey, I just saw your text. I'm headed back to the house now," she informed him.

Keece continued to grip Alyssa's waist with one of his hands. "Shit...Okay, I'll see you later," he spoke, feeling his nut approaching.

"Damn, Daddy, you hitting my spot," Alyssa moaned loudly.

Keece snapped out of his sex-induced haze and gave her a look that could kill. He would never want to disrespect Paris and let her hear him having sex with another woman. If Alyssa wasn't riding him like a pro, he would've slapped the shit out of her.

"Who the fuck was *that*?" Paris quizzed.

"Nobody," he quickly replied.

"You're fucking lying! I know your ass ain't fucking while you're on the phone with me! You a nasty-ass bastard!" Paris yelled and hung up the phone.

Keece threw his phone in the passenger's seat and continued to ram his nine inches into Alyssa's wet tunnel. Minutes later, Keece filled the condom with semen while Alyssa's fluids coated the condom. She got up slowly and climbed back to the passenger's seat. Keece threw the condom out of the window and buckled his pants.

"Who was that on the phone?" Alyssa asked.

"Why?" he responded, irritated.

"Because you never tell me to be quiet when you're on the phone."

Keece started his car without paying her any attention. "It was nobody."

"Well, I'm cooking tonight, and I want you to come over. You think you can make it happen? We haven't spent time together in weeks."

Keece gave her a look and then stared at his phone. She had truly pissed him off, and he felt it had been done on purpose. Keece had already made up in his mind that he wouldn't be joining her for dinner.

"Yeah, I'll come," he lied.

Alyssa clapped her hands happily. "Really? Okay, here is the key to my house. If I'm not there, just make yourself at home."

"Why wouldn't you be there?" Keece quizzed.

"Because I'll probably be at the grocery store. Look, I gotta get back to work. Thanks for the release, Daddy." Alyssa kissed his cheek and then hopped out of the car.

Keece tried calling Paris back, but he was sent to the voicemail. He knew she was going to have an attitude with him because he was for sure fucking while on the phone with her. Although they weren't a couple, he still had a lot of respect for her. And he didn't want to hurt her feelings.

Keece mentally prepared for the night ahead because he knew Paris was going to be throwing a lot of shade.

CHAPTER SIXTEEN

Later that evening, Paris found herself at Camara's house playing with baby Milan. Rochelle had prepared some jambalaya for dinner, and Aimee had made her famous Patron margaritas. Paris couldn't remember the last time she'd enjoyed girl time and alcohol. Moments like this made her miss her life before the rape. Even though she had been making progress in moving past her trauma, she still missed the carefree side of life.

"So Keece was actually fucking while he was talking to you?" Camara asked.

Paris scoffed before she sipped on her margarita, "Yes, with his nasty ass. He made me so mad," she said getting upset all over again.

"At least he answered your call though, right?" Aimee added.

Paris gave her a look that said, "Bitch please!"

"How would you like it if Big's chocolate ass called you fucking in the background?"

Aimee gave her a side eye. "Listen, please don't make the crazy side of me start showing. I will literally kill his ass. As a matter of fact, let me call and make sure everything is good." She grabbed her phone and left out of the room.

Paris, Camara, and Rochelle all shared a laugh because Aimee's personality went from nice girl to around the way girl within seconds. Paris' phone began to ring, and she noticed that it was Keece calling for the umpteenth time. She politely hit decline and continued bouncing Milan on her knee. She knew Keece would be worried because it was almost ten o'clock at night, and she had yet to return to his home.

"Was that Keece calling?" Camara asked.

Paris plastered an evil smile on her face. "Yep. He'll probably be calling your phone in a minute."

"Girl, you better stop playing with my son's emotions. You know he'll tear up the city if he has to," Rochelle teased Paris.

Minutes later, Aimee returned to the room and sat down. They all looked at her and started laughing. Eventually, she laughed too. Big had hung up on her because she wanted to know the name of every person she'd heard in the background. Camara's ringing phone interrupted their laughing session. She picked it up and showed Paris the screen.

It was Keece.

"Don't answer, Paris pleaded.

Camara ignored her and answered the phone. "Hey, Keece... Yeah, she's here...Okay, we'll be here." Camara hung up the phone and looked at Paris.

Paris frowned at her. "Why did you do that? I should go upstairs and tell Kiyan how you used to steal money out of his pants pockets," Paris threatened.

"I know you weren't stealing from my boy!" Rochelle yelled dramatically.

Paris nodded. "Yes, she was. Then she would come get me to go shopping. She ain't shit."

"He used to make me mad. So I would charge him for that shit. He knew. Don't think he didn't," Camara said, waving them off.

Minutes later, the doorbell rang, and Rochelle got up to answer. Camara and Aimee snickered at each other because they knew Keece would walk in at any minute. Paris rolled her eyes at the two and began to count to ten. She knew Keece was about to put on a show because she'd been ignoring him.

"Why aren't you answering my calls?" Keece barked, entering the room.

Before she could look in his direction, his Giorgio Armani cologne hit her nose. He stood there looking like a Calvin Klein model wearing a fresh white T-shirt, Balmain jeans, and retro Jordan's. His fresh cut framed his face perfectly, and his beard accentuated his square jaw line.

Paris offered him an uninterested look. "I didn't hear my phone ringing."

Keece walked over to her and removed the baby from her arms. Milan smiled and drooled when Keece kissed her on the cheek.

"So, Keece, I heard you was getting it in today while you were on the phone talking to my girl. What's up with that?" Camara instigated, causing Aimee to giggle.

Keece looked down at Paris and shook his head. "How did you know I was fucking? I could've been doing something else," he argued.

Paris huffed. "Keece please don't play with me. Ol' girl said you were hitting her spot. Now tell me what spot you were hitting."

"I was hooking her up with clippers. You know how sensitive the back of the neck can be," he joked.

Everyone busted out laughing, except for Paris, who obviously found no humor in his statement. She shook head and walked out of the living room. Since her cup was empty, she headed to the kitchen. Keece passed the baby to his mom and followed Paris to the kitchen. He felt bad because he knew her feelings were hurt. He really didn't have to explain anything to Paris since they weren't together, but she was still his baby, and he didn't want to cause her any more pain.

Keece stood closely behind her as she poured her drink. "You mad?"

Paris rolled her eyes. "Mad for what? You're not my man, right?"

"Right. But you seem a little upset, though. What can I do to make you feel better?" he asked while massaging her shoulders.

Paris shrugged him off. "You don't have to do anything. I'm good, Keece,"

Paris turned around and faced him. He had a silly grin plastered on his face that she wanted to smack off. She could tell that he was enjoying her obvious jealousy, so she decided to get him back.

She smirked. "I found a place, so I'll be out of your house in a couple of weeks. Thanks for your hospitality."

Instantly, Keece's grin faded after the words she'd just spoken settled in. He had begun to feel comfortable with Paris being in his company again. Coming home every night was exciting for Keece because he knew Paris was there waiting for him. There was no way he was going to let her move out. He refused to allow her to take the risk of being hurt by Chase again. He wouldn't be able to sleep knowing she was all alone.

Keece twisted his face. "What do you mean you found a place? Why are you trying to leave?"

Paris found his sudden change of attitude amusing. "I think it's time for me to move on with my life and get back to doing me. Plus, I've overstayed my welcome, don't you think?" she asked innocently.

Keece shook his head, attempting to calm himself down. "Paris, you on that bullshit. You know you can stay as long as you want to. And what you mean by move on? I hope you're not trying to find another nigga!" The vein on the side of his neck throbbed as he envisioned Paris being with another man.

Paris cocked her head to the side. "Oh, so you can answer the phone while fucking some other chick, but I can't date another man? What part of the game is that, Keece?

You have a girlfriend. Don't you think I may want to find a boyfriend?"

"Man, that bitch ain't my girlfriend! And no, you shouldn't be trying to find no boyfriend. We're not ready for that now."

"*We're* not ready? Um... Excuse me? Can you clarify that please?" Paris asked dramatically, cupping her ear with her hand so she could hear him clearly.

Keece stepped closer to her and put his lips to her ear. "Paris, why are you trying to act like you're not mine? You know who you belong to," he whispered in her ear.

Paris closed her eyes as her body shuddered from his words. Keece had always had the ability to make her weak at any given moment, and she hated that. Quickly gathering herself, she took a step back.

"Whatever, Keece. You say that, but you were knee-deep in someone else's kitty cat earlier," she said and walked out of the room.

Keece watch her fat ass jiggle as she exited the room. At that moment, he mentally declared that he would have Paris back into his life permanently. With him is where she belonged. Keece knew it, and Paris did too. The love they once shared for each other was still present. No one would take Paris' place, in his eyes. She had a hold on his heart that no one would ever be able to break. She was his everything, and he promised to do right by her this time around.

****

A couple of days later, Keece pulled up to Dinero's car wash. He needed to drop some money off so it could be counted. Plus, he hadn't heard from him in over a week, which was unusual. But Keece knew the reason why. Every time Dinero became upset, he would disappear for weeks until someone came to check on him. Keece had always found himself in this situation when it came to his brother. Since he was his big brother, Keece was expected to make the first move.

He walked inside of the car wash and was greeted by Meesha and Terri. They were two eighteen-year-old girls from around the way that Dinero had hired. They were pretty cool chicks, and they stayed out of trouble most of the time. Whenever they were asked to count the money for Keece, their numbers were always right.

"Hey, Keece, what's goin' on, fam?" Meesha asked, giving him a handshake.

"Nothing. What's up with y'all? How're those report cards looking?"

They looked at each other as if in deep thought. "They're cool. I got like a 3.5 GPA, and Terri's got a 3.0," Meesha responded.

"Yeah, Keece, we're still keeping up with our school work. Don't worry," Terri assured him.

Keece nodded. "That's good. Aye, I need y'all to count this money for me. But I'll give it to Dinero. Where's he at?"

"He's in his office. We got you."

Keece walked off, headed toward the back, and knocked on Dinero's door. Once he was granted access, he found his brother sitting behind his desk zipping up his pants. Seconds later, a female popped up, looking embarrassed. She quickly made her exit. Keece shook his head and let out a hearty laugh.

"Bro, you wild as fuck. Ain't that one of your workers?" Keece asked, taking a seat.

Dinero smiled.. "Yep. Aye, she offered, and you know a nigga like me wasn't turning down shit but my collar," he said, adjusting the collar on his shirt.

Keece laughed and threw the duffle bag full of money on the floor.

"It needs to be counted?" Dinero asked.

Keece took a seat on the sofa. "Yeah. I already let Meesha and Terri know."

"I've been meaning to talk to you," Dinero said, sitting on top of his desk.

"Oh yeah? About what?"

"Listen, I know I go about shit in a different way than you do, and at times I make bad decisions. Keece, I understand that you've bailed me out of a lot of situations, and I appreciate it. Bro, my intentions are always good. I don't be fucking up on purpose. I guess I try to prove myself to you because I've learned a lot of shit from you. Shit, I didn't even watch Pops make moves like I watch you do. That's real shit. You inspire me. That's why I'm trying to get my shit together, so I won't make any more bad decisions. But don't hold that shit against me 'cause I'm trying to do right."

Dinero had never spoken to Keece on a level so personal and was anxiously awaiting his reply.

Keece was shocked by Dinero's words. He'd always known that Dinero looked up to him, but he had never expressed it to him. He didn't want his brother making moves in order to prove himself because he didn't have to. Keece had meant it when he told his brothers that they were in this together.

Talking with Dinero made Keece realize that leaving their drug operation wasn't the best decision at the moment.

Kiyan was right. They'd all taken an oath that they would always get money together, and Keece didn't want to break that vow just yet.

He scooted to the edge of his chair, saying, "Look, man, I'm not holding anything against you. I just want you to be smart about everything. You don't have to prove shit to me. I know you're capable of making the best moves for our business because you've done it in the past. Listen, I promise not to bring up that shit with Dyno anymore, a'ight? Let's just get back to making this money." Keece stood up and walked over to Dinero, and they shared a brotherly hug.

"I'm over this mushy shit. Let's go meet Big at the bar," Dinero suggested.

"Cool. Come on."

****

Big was posted at his bar when Dom arrived to pay him a visit. It was rare for his father to come to the bar, but since his relationship with his son's had gone sour, he was doing a lot of things out of the norm. Despite his brothers' decisions not to deal with Dom on a regular basis, Big still kept in touch with him. In his eyes, he was still his father, and even though he had done some foul things to his brothers, Big would never cut him off.

Dom had rescued Big when he was in need of a stable place to live. His mother had been struggling with alcohol, which was due to his biological father's death. She wasn't able to take care of him. So with her permission, Dom stepped in and took Big into his home. He had treated him no differently than he'd done his own boys. And for that, Big would always be indebted to him.

"What's up, Pops?" Big greeted him with a hug.

Dom looked well dressed in his signature Tom Ford suit. He still kept his hair cut low with his salt and pepper goatee lined to perfection.

"I can't call it. What's been going on in your world?" he asked, taking a seat at the bar.

Big shrugged. "Same shit, different day. What do you want to drink?"

"I'll take a shot Hennessey."

Big called his bartender over and told her to get Dom a shot of Hennessey. Dom couldn't help but stare at the busty lady with shoulder length hair.

Big noticed his lustful stares and chuckled. "You like what you see?"

Dom nodded as he bit his lip. "Man, do I. I'm loving this single shit. I don't have to deal with a woman if I don't want to. I can get the pussy and kick her ass out." He laughed.

"So you're really done with Celine, Pops? Y'all were married for a long-ass time. I always saw y'all as the perfect couple," Big told him.

Dom shifted in his seat before responding. "Well, as you can see, that shit was all based on a lie, and I was dumb enough to have believed the shit. Celine fucked up, but I did too. There ain't no way we can stay together after all of this shit."

Big nodded, agreeing with him. "I feel you. How does Case feel about all of this?"

Dom took a sip of his drink and shrugged. "He hasn't said too much. I believe he's trying to stay neutral and out of the mix. But I'm sure it bothers him. It's out of my hands, you know?"

Silence filled the air as Dom thought about his broken family. They used to be such a close-knit bunch, but now they barely even called each other.

"How have your brothers been?" Dom asked.

"They're cool. Ain't nothing new going on. Oh, I forgot to tell you that Keece is about to open up a tattoo shop," Big announced proudly.

"For real? That might be a good move for him. He's talented with that kind of shit."

Dom sipped on his drink and smiled on the inside. He'd always told Keece that tattooing would make him very rich, but he had put his dreams on hold to run the family business.

Dom turned and looked at Big, "So what's up with you and this new girl? You like her, don't you?" he asked with a smirk.

Big was caught off guard by the question because he'd been private and reserved about his feelings for Aimee. But since it was *Dom* asking, he decided to open up to him. "Yeah, that's my lil' lady. She's cool as shit, but you know I've got to keep her on the low from Tara. I don't want her to run Aimee off." Big shook his head as he thought about his baby mama and her antics.

"Tara just needs her ass whooped real good. She would never pull that bullshit on me," Dom scoffed and then looked at his watch.

He stood up and put his jacket back on, saying, "Aye, I gotta head out. I have a meeting with my realtor. I'll talk to you later."

He hugged Big before he walked out of the bar. As he headed to his car, he spotted Keece and Dinero. He hadn't seen them since he was in the hospital. He'd truly been missing them. The feeling was foreign to Dom because they had always been close.

"How're y'all doing?" Dom asked, walking up to them.

"I'm good. What's up with you?" Keece asked.

Dinero decided to give a head nod instead of respond.

"I'm better. Tell Kiyan that I've been calling him, and it would be nice if he would return my call," Dom said sternly.

"I'll relay the message, Pops," Keece said, smirking.

Dinero tried so desperately to hold in his laugh but found it difficult when he looked over at Keece.

Dom shook his head. "I'll talk to y'all goofy asses later." He chuckled and walked off.

After Dom walked away, Keece and Dinero busted out laughing. They had told Kiyan numerous times to call their father back, and his reply was always, "Fuck his bitch ass."

They finally walked into the bar and spotted Big in the back near the pool tables.

"What's up, bro?" Keece greeted him.

"Shit, y'all just missed Pops," Big informed them.

"We saw him in the parking lot. What the fuck was he doing up in here? His ass don't ever come to the bar," Dinero wanted to know as he grabbed a pool stick.

"I guess he wanted to holla at me. Where are y'all coming from?" Big asked, changing the subject.

"We just left the car wash. Did you talk to Kiyan today?" Keece asked.

Big shook his head before downing his drink. "Nah. I think he took Camara out of town for the weekend. Aye, but

I heard your ass got caught up the other day. How you gon' answer the phone fucking, my nigga?"

Keece shook his head because he knew nobody but Aimee had told Big about the incident. Not only had he been forced to deal with Paris, but now he had to hear his brothers clown him about the situation.

Dinero looked at Keece, not believing his ears. "What? You rookie as fuck." He laughed.

Keece laughed and shook his head. He hated whenever they ganged up on him.

"Listen, I didn't want to miss her call just in case she was in trouble. I told Alyssa's fool ass to be quiet, but that bitch started moaning and shit. She pissed me off," Keece ranted.

"Man, you knew she wasn't gon' stay quiet. You just wanted to make Paris mad," Big said, calling him out.

Keece twisted his face, annoyed by Big's comment. "Come on. You know I wouldn't do no hoe shit like that," he snapped.

"Aye, what's up with you and Paris, though?" Dinero asked. "How is she doing after all that shit that happened to her?"

"She's better. She's not walking around looking sad and shit. Y'all still ain't found his bitch ass?" Keece asked Big.

"Hell nah. That nigga got ghost. The address you gave us has been vacant ever since the shit happened. I bet his ass skipped town," Big said.

"For his sake, I hope he did, 'cause when I find him I'ma murk his bitch ass." Keece felt his phone vibrate inside of his pocket so he took it out. He noticed that it was Alyssa texting him. Ever since he'd stood her up the other night, she had been calling and texting nonstop. Every time Keece told her that he would call her back, she'd end up following up with him instead.

Keece opened her message.

From: Alyssa

U think u can come over today? I miss u.

Keece instantly messaged her back.

To: Alyssa

Nah, not today.

Keece put his phone away and picked up a pool stick. He started a game with Big. They jumped into a conversation about their plans to expand. Keece also informed him that he had decided not to leave their drug operation just yet. Big and Dinero were elated about the news. He did explain to them that he still wanted to open his tattoo shop. Keece felt his phone vibrate again and saw that it was none other than Alyssa.

Keece sucked his teeth as he hit the ignore button. "Aye, I'm about to stop fucking with Alyssa's ass. She's too fucking clingy for me. She acts like I sit on my ass all day and don't have anything to do. All she wanna do is sit in my face all day. I need a bitch that can go on about her own fucking business."

"Damn, and to think I wanted to smash. It ain't worth it, huh?" Dinero asked.

"Nah, the pussy ain't worth all the whining, phone calls, and texts. But to each his own. I'm about to go holla at her ass real quick. I'ma get up with y'all later."

Keece decided it was time to end things with Alyssa. His mind was now set on getting back together with Paris, and he knew he wouldn't be able to pull it off with Alyssa still in the background. Plus, Keece felt like Alyssa's feelings were becoming stronger for him while his feelings lie elsewhere.

He hopped in his car and made his way to Alyssa's house. She lived pretty close to Big's bar, so he made it there in no time. He grabbed the spare key that Alyssa had given him days before and exited the car. He walked to her door, unlocked it, and entered the house quietly, closing the door behind him.

"Alyssa!" Keece called out.

He walked toward the back in the direction of her bedroom, where he heard muffled sounds. The closer he got, the slower he moved. From what he could hear, Alyssa was crying on the phone. Keece stopped in his tracks when he heard her say his name.

"I'm trying to, Shy, but he hasn't been feeling me lately... I did. I invited him over a few nights ago, but he never showed up."

Keece continued to eavesdrop, because something didn't feel right about her conversation, and the fact that she was speaking about him infuriated him more.

"Lil Ron was here waiting for him so he could pull it off. I told you I didn't feel comfortable trying to set Keece up. I don't wanna do this anymore, Shy. It's not right," she cried.

What the fuck? Keece thought to himself.

He couldn't believe his own ears. Alyssa had been playing him the entire time, trying to set him up. Instantly, a switch went off within Keece. He burst into the room.

"Who're you on the phone with?" Keece bellowed, obviously startling Alyssa.

She dropped the phone and turned around to see Keece standing there with his fist balled up. Her heartbeat could be felt in her throat as her body started to shake viciously. She wondered how long he had been standing there and how much of her conversation he'd heard.

Alyssa tucked her hair behind her ear nervously, "Hey, um...Keece, what are you doing here?" she asked, trying to sound normal.

Keece walked toward her slowly. "Bitch, you tried to set me up? Is that why your ass has been hawking me? Is it because you're trying to help someone rob me?"

"Wait! I can explain," she pleaded.

Keece rushed Alyssa to the floor and climbed on top of her. Her screams echoed throughout the room as Keece's strong hands grabbed hold of her neck and squeezed. She was terrified of what was to come.

"You dumb bitch! You would never be able to set up a man like me, you fool-ass bitch," he yelled with spittle flying out of his mouth.

Keece smacked Alyssa hard on her face, causing her lip to bleed instantly. She kicked and screamed for dear life, but it was to no avail. She had never seen Keece's eyes so cold, and it scared her to death. She wanted to explain to him that she'd changed her mind about setting him up, but at that moment, Alyssa knew it would fall on deaf ears.

"Keece..." Alyssa gasped, clawing at his hands.

"Keece what? Oh, now you want to talk? Fuck you! I'm about to end your hoe-ass life," he gritted.

Keece applied more pressure to her neck, which caused her eyeballs to bulge from their sockets. Alyssa tried her best to escape Keece's strong grasp, but she was no match for his strength. Tears began to slip from her eyes because she knew death was approaching. Keece watched as Alyssa's life slowly began to fade away. His grip was so strong around her neck that his fingernails dug deep into her skin.

Seconds later, Alyssa's body fell limp. After making sure Alyssa was dead, Keece stood up and looked around for her phone. When he spotted it, he picked it up and grabbed his phone out of his pocket. Keece made sure to store the number of the last person she'd spoken with in his phone before he held it up to his ear.

"Alyssa, baby...Hello?" the caller spoke in a panic.

"Alyssa can't come to the phone right now," Keece said and hung up, making sure to put her phone in his pocket.

It had been a while since he had caught a body. He did his best to avoid situations such as this. But there was no way that Keece could've allowed Alyssa to walk away, knowing she had tried to set him up. There was no telling how many people she'd set up in the past.

Keece hurried and dialed Big's number.

He answered on the third ring. "What's up, bro?"

"Aye, I need you to meet me at this address I'm about to text you. I need help taking out the garbage."

CHAPTER SEVENTEEN

One week later...

Paris sat at desk shopping online. She had become bored and decided to indulge in a little retail therapy to cheer herself up. Camara had gone out of town with Kiyan, and Aimee was busy with her sister. Her trusted employee had offered to get her out of the house, but Paris didn't think that clubbing was the right move for her at the time. Her paranoia was decreasing, but it hadn't totally disappeared. Feeling parched, Paris got up to head to the kitchen. She noticed that Keece's room was empty as she walked past it. Wondering where he was, she dialed his number.

"Hello?"

She grabbed a bottle of water out of the fridge, saying, "Hey, I was calling to find out where you were."

"I had to make a last-minute trip to New York," he informed her.

Paris sucked her teeth. "Why didn't you tell me? You know I don't like staying in this house by myself. I would've gone to my mom's place," she fussed.

"You'll be fine. Just set the alarm."

"Yeah...whatever. I see your communication skills are still fucked up. Goodbye!" she shot and hung up.

Paris took the staircase up to the second level of the house. When she reached the landing, Keece popped out and scared her, causing her to screech. "Arrgh!"

He belted out a laugh and held his stomach.

"You're such an ass! Why would you do that?" Paris yelled, throwing punches at him.

He grabbed her hands to keep her from hitting him. "I couldn't help it."

"Ooh! You get on my nerves. How long have you been here?" she asked.

"For a minute. Why? Did you miss me?" He grinned.

Paris cut her eyes at him. "Hell no, I didn't miss your ignorant ass. Now move out of my way."

Paris tried to walk past Keece, but he hurried and scooped her up and threw her over his shoulder. Paris protested weakly, as he carried her to his bedroom. Keece kicked the door shut and threw Paris on the bed.

"Who said I wanna be in here with you?" Paris spat, secretly happy to be in the same room as Keece.

"*I* did. Now lay your ass back," Keece replied and joined her on the bed.

Paris laid back as she watched Keece grab the remote and search through the channels. Keece lay there, unaware that Paris was watching him. His skin smelled fresh, as if he had just stepped out of the shower, and his miniature hills were begging to be licked. She and Keece hadn't been intimate in several months, and just the thought of his sexual performances made Paris become aroused.

"What are you thinking about Paris?" Keece asked, snatching her from her naughty thoughts.

Paris quickly cleared her throat. "Um...nothing."

"Come closer to me," he instructed, holding up his arm.

Paris scooted closer and she laid her head on his chest. Being this close to him created a familiar comfort that she'd missed. She closed her eyes and inhaled his body scent. Paris could feel her kitty cat begin to get wet, which caught her by surprise.

"So where are you trying to move to?" he asked while raking his fingers through her hair.

"Maybe the Washington Heights area. I'm not sure." Paris couldn't concentrate on anything he was saying because she was in such a trance.

He looked down at her. "You know you don't have to move. You can stay here with me."

"I know, Keece, but I think it's time to go. Plus, I don't want your girlfriend to become upset." She smirked.

Keece exhaled loudly. "I don't have a girlfriend. So stop bringing that shit up. You must be jealous. Are you jealous, Paris?" he taunted her.

"Why would I be jealous when I've already had you, Keece?"

Keece gave her a look and shook his head. He was tired of Paris trying to act like she was unbothered with everything. It was time for Keece to show her that he was still the nigga that got whatever he wanted. At that moment, Paris was what he desired the most.

Keece sat up, rolled over, and positioned himself between Paris' legs. Surprisingly, she didn't resist him. She actually opened her legs further, allowing him better access. Keece looked deep into her eyes, causing Paris' breathing to become shallow. He kissed her lips gently and slipped his tongue inside of her mouth. Paris' hands found the back of his head and started rubbing it lovingly as Keece made love to her mouth. She anxiously awaited any negative thoughts about the rape that might ruin the moment, but none surfaced.

Keece trailed kisses to her neck and began licking and biting it gently. He knew when he was done with her neck, that she would have a few passion marks. Paris bit her bottom lip, as her body temperature began to rise. His fingers found her nipple. He pinched and rubbed it until it became hard. Without warning, Keece hungrily consumed each breast, sucking her nipples alternately. By now, Paris' pussy was throbbing and begging for Keece to enter it.

Tired of the teasing, Keece snatched Paris' thongs off and then threw her legs over his shoulders. Before diving into her kitty, Keece gave her a look that said, "I'm about to have you screaming."

Seconds later, Keece's tongue found her moist middle and he began to write his name in it. His touch created a euphoric sensation that caused Paris to squirm. He was breaking down the walls that she had so desperately tried to keep up. Keece latched onto her clit and sucked the life out of it. It didn't take long for Paris legs to start shaking.

"Keece...Shit..." Paris whimpered, feeling her orgasm draw near.

Seconds later, Paris creamed all over Keece's mouth, making him to smile. Keece took his fingers and smeared her juices all over her pussy. He grabbed her legs and scooted her closer to him. Then Keece plunged his thick penis deep into Paris. She gasped in response. He filled up her insides, stretching her so wide that he knew she wouldn't have any walls when he was finished with her.

"Now let's talk," he said in a husky voice with his lips touching hers.

Keece pulled all the way out and then thrust deep into Paris again. He was trying to send her a message that nobody would be able to please her body like he could.

"You gon' stop playing and come back to Daddy?" Keece asked, pulling out.

"Keece, stop playing and put it back in," Paris begged, feeling like a mad woman.

"Answer the question," he said biting her ear.

"Yes, Daddy, I will. Now put it back in," she purred.

Keece happily obliged and dived deep into her ocean. Paris locked her legs around his waist just in case he felt like playing games again.

"You still love me, Paris?" Keece asked, attacking her G-spot.

Her eyes began to roll like The Undertaker. "Oh, my God. Yes, I do," she professed.

Keece kissed her lips and began thrusting his hips in a circular motion. Paris yelled out in pure bliss as he found areas of her pussy that she didn't know existed.

"You gon' give me another chance, baby?" he asked, feeling the tip of his dick tingle.

Paris moaned loudly as Keece murdered her pussy. "Yes, baby. Ooh...right there!" she yelled.

That was all Keece needed to hear as he sat up on his knees and placed her legs in the crook of his arms. Paris was so wet that he could hear her juices splash after every stroke. Keece could stay inside of her pussy all night if he could. That's how great it felt.

"I'm about to cum," Paris announced, feeling like she was under a spell.

Keece picked up his pace as he dug deeper into her sex. Minutes later, he released his load of semen inside of Paris while she rained fluids all over his dick. Out of breath, Keece fell over on the side of Paris, trying to regulate his breathing. Paris hadn't realized how backed up she'd been. She appreciated Keece for relaxing her body.

"I wore your ass out." Keece laughed.

Paris was still spent, so she smiled at him and shook her head. She would be lying if she said that Keece hadn't put it down. She snuggled up to him and lowered her guard. There would never be another man who would make her as happy as Keece did. Even though he hadn't been honest in the past, Paris felt in her heart that he would do things differently this time. She could feel the change in him. He would take better care of her heart from this day forward.

"I love you, baby," he told her before he kissed her forehead.

"I love you too."

****

A couple days later, Keece sat in his barbershop, along with Dinero and Big, chatting with all of the on-duty barbers. It was their usual hangout spot on Fridays before getting into their evening activities. It was always loud because of the normal heated debates over miscellaneous topics.

"So you're telling me that LeBron is better than Jordan?" Big asked Rob, one of the barbers.

"When he gets done with his career, his stats will be better than Jordan's," Rob stated.

Dinero waved his hand dismissively. "Fuck outta here. Jordan will always be the G.O.A.T.," he countered.

"CP, what do you think?" Rob asked the manager of the shop.

CP had been the manager and also Keece's barber for about three years. Keece trusted him with his business and his lining.

"Man, I don't care about that basketball bullshit. Fuck them rich niggas," CP returned with a laugh.

Rob waved him off and then continued to cut his client's hair.

"What are y'all getting into tonight? I'll probably hit up Onyx," CP asked Keece and Big.

Big shrugged. "Shit, I'll probably kick it with my lady tonight. She's been on my back about spending more time with her."

"Aimee's on that bullshit?" Keece joked.

Big grinned. "Man, you know how it is. I'm not used to this relationship shit, but I'm not gon' complain, though. That's my baby."

"Niggas are all in love and shit," CP said, clowning Big.

"When you get the right one it be like that. You should try it, nigga," Keece shot.

CP smirked. "Nah, I ain't knocking it. I had a bitch that I thought I could fuck with, but she ended up playing me in the end," he revealed.

"How?" Dinero asked.

CP shook his head. "Man, it's a long-ass story. It's one you wouldn't believe if you heard it," he said and wrapped up his clippers.

The door chimed, and in walked Kiyan, looking as if he'd had a tan. He had been missing in action for the last couple days, since he'd taken Camara to Miami for the weekend. Big had called and told him that they had something to tell him, and Kiyan couldn't wait to touch down back in Milwaukee.

"The shop is closed," Keece joked.

Kiyan held his middle finger up. "Fuck you! My plane just landed like an hour ago. I'm tired as fuck," he complained while shaking up with everybody.

"Man, your ol' step-in-the-name-of-love ass been caking like a mothafucka," Dinero joked.

Kiyan laughed. "Shut up, fuck boy."

"So was there a lot of bad bitches down there?" Big asked.

Kiyan shook his head as he groaned. "Man, you don't understand what kind of pressure I was under. Those hoes were so thick and beautiful. Every time I tried to sneak a peek, Camara's crazy ass threatened me and shit..." Kiyan laughed.

"You know Camara don't play that shit. Aye, but we gotta fill you in on some shit. Let's go to the office," Keece suggested.

Kiyan, Big, and Dinero followed Keece to his office area. It was more like a lounge with two large couches and a 55-inch flat screen TV. Dinero made sure the door was shut before he joined his brothers on the couch.

"Man, Big called me and told me some shit went down. What the fuck happened?" Kiyan inquired.

Keece rested his hand on his forehead as he spoke. "Bro, I had to off that bitch, Alyssa. That hoe was trying to set me up to get robbed," he spat, getting upset all over again.

"What? How did you figure that shit out?" Kiyan asked, in disbelief of Keece's words.

Keece told him about the entire scene at Alyssa's home, as well as the phone call. Kiyan couldn't believe what he'd heard. He had never picked up on any shady behavior from Alyssa at all.

"Oh, Big, did you get any info on that number I gave you?" Keece asked him.

Keece had given Big the number that was on Alyssa's phone and told him to trace it. Big had a chick that worked at the police station he fucked with from time to time. She would always come through on information that they couldn't get since she had the resources.

"Man, she told me it was a burn out phone. Ain't no way to trace it," Big informed Keece.

Keece frowned. "Fuck! All I know is she kept calling him Shy. I'm sure it's like a nickname or some shit," he said, shaking his head.

"I bet he was the nigga that was the mastermind behind all of that shit. We gotta find out who he is before he sends somebody else to get at you," Dinero spoke.

"Whoever he is ain't about to catch me slipping again. I can promise you that shit," Keece spat.

"I'll ask some of my lil' homies if they know anybody named Shy. They usually know everybody. Now you gotta watch out for *everybody*. No more new bitches. Stick to the ones you know," Kiyan joked.

"Fuck that! I ain't fucking with no hoes *period*," Keece declared.

Dinero snickered. "We'll see how long that last," he challenged.

"It's about to last a long time 'cause I'm trying to lock Paris down again. This situation made me realize these hoes really ain't shit."

"So you tryin' to get that old thing back, huh? I ain't mad at you, 'cause Paris is a bad bitch. I should've got at her the night she came to the club," Dinero said, stroking his goatee.

Keece glared at him, ready to slap the shit out of him. "Dinero, you tryin' to get fucked up by commenting on my bitch?"

Kiyan and Big erupted in laughter, causing Dinero to laugh as well. Dinero had always thought Paris was

KEECE AND PARIS 2

beautiful, but he would never cross that line. Plus, he enjoyed pissing Keece off since he knew he was crazy in love with Paris.

Dinero continued pushing Keece's button. "I'm just saying, my nigga. She's beautiful as hell."

"I know this and?" Keece continued to glare at him.

After a brief staring match, Keece finally laughed, breaking the ice. He would never take Dinero serious when it came to Paris, but if it was anybody else, he wouldn't hesitate to check them.

"Dude be doing the same shit with Aimee. I gotta watch your ass," Big said, pointing at Dinero.

Dinero smiled devilishly. "Now Aimee can get—"

"Aye, don't play with me for real," Big said, cutting him off.

They all laughed and continued discussing the search for the guy named Shy. Keece didn't want to dwell on the Alyssa situation, but he knew that he wouldn't be able rest peacefully until he'd found this Shy character.

CHAPTER EIGHTEEN

Paris sat on the phone with her friend Tony. They had gone to high school together and managed to stay in contact over the years. It had been months since they'd last talked to each other, and Paris couldn't deny that she'd missed her dear friend. He had no idea what Paris had been through the last couple months, so she filled him in.

"Damn, Paris, I'm glad your ass survived that shit. Do you know what they do to people who are sold into human trafficking? I watched a documentary on it a while back, and that shit is terrible."

"I know. You don't even know how many times a day I thank God. I could've been raped on a daily basis or maybe even drugged." Paris sighed.

"Man, I would've been fucked up if you had gone missing. But you're good now, though, right?" he asked.

"I'm a lot better now. I'm not as paranoid as before, but I'm still on guard. I have to give credit to my family and friends because they've helped me on this journey."

Paris heard her door crack open and saw Keece poke his head in. He was wearing his signature grin with his eyes glazed over from smoking. Paris smiled as she watched him watching her.

"Who are you on the phone with?" Keece asked, looking at her with so much intensity that she felt like a child being scolded by her father.

"My friend..."

"Who?" Keece said, making his way toward her.

"Tony, I'm gon' call you later, okay? Bye." Paris said all in one breath.

"It better have been a chick named Toni and not a fucking dude named Tony," Keece snapped.

Paris hurried and locked her phone before Keece could grab it. Once he snatched it, he tried to unlock it, but he couldn't. Paris watched him, snickering because he was frustrated that he couldn't get inside of her phone.

"Why are you being sneaky, Paris? Who the fuck is Tony?"

"He's my friend from high school. Keece, don't come in here acting like you're a detective and shit. He's just my *friend*," Paris argued, walking into the bathroom.

"You don't need any more friends. You already got Camara and Aimee. I don't want to catch you on the phone with him no more either."

Paris walked out of the bathroom and stared at Keece. He was getting undressed with a frown on his face. She wanted to laugh because he looked so cute when he was mad. Keece grabbed a blunt and headed out on the balcony. Paris threw her robe on and followed him. He sat down, took out his lighter, and lit the blunt. Paris watched him as he inhaled and exhaled the kush.

It seemed like with each passing day, Paris fell deeper in love with Keece. It had only been a week ago that she'd contemplated moving out of his home. Now, she couldn't fathom spending a day without him. The table had turned so quickly for Paris, but it was all for the better. She knew without a doubt that Keece loved her and would give his life to ensure that she was safe.

"Keecey...Isn't that what your mom calls you?" she chuckled.

"That shit sounds gay," Keece said, shaking his head.

"What? I think it's cute. I think I might start calling you Keecey Pooh." She laughed.

"Don't do that, Paris," he warned.

"Do what?"

"Don't call me that bullshit and don't be on the phone with other niggas. I don't like that shit," he fussed.

"Listen, don't come in here giving out any demands. Did you end things with your fuck buddy? Are you and Riley still in contact? Let's talk about that shit," Paris quipped, looking him square in the eyes.

Keece laughed at her because she had just displayed a calm demeanor only a minute ago, but now she was rolling her neck and giving him attitude.

"Riley? Man, you definitely don't have to worry about Riley anymore. I haven't spoken to her in months. She's old news. You don't have to worry about the fuck buddy either. I got rid of her." Keece chuckled because he'd meant it *literally*.

"Yeah, you better had. I'm not sharing you anymore, do you hear me, Keece? I'll walk away and never look back at your ass," she threatened.

"You'll never have to share me again. I promise," he assured her before he gave her a passionate kiss.

Paris loved the feel of his full lips against hers. She pulled back with a smile on her face.

"Oh, I want to talk to you about something," she spoke.

"What?"

"I've decided to go back to work. And before you say anything, I want you to know that I've found a new office.

There'll be a security guard inside of my office, as well as one downstairs. I've taken enough time off of work, and it's time to get back to doing me. Plus, people have been calling, inquiring about my services, and I don't want to miss any more money."

Keece groaned on the inside because if it were up to him, Paris would take more time off. The fact that her rapist was still on the run frustrated him, and he didn't want her to risk getting hurt again. Keece wanted to protest, but he knew that Paris loved being a lawyer. He couldn't force her to give up her career no matter what.

"I don't like it," Keece said honestly.

"I knew you wouldn't approve, but I need your support. I promise you I'm good. Every day I feel myself becoming stronger emotionally and mentally. I can handle this," Paris ensured as she stroked his strong back.

Keece sat for a moment before he responded. "A'ight. I'll try my best to support you, but you gotta have a driver to take you back and forth to work. Oh, and you gotta call me *every* hour."

"Every hour? What if I'm in court, Keece," Paris asked, giving him a side eye.

"Yeah, I want you to hit me up every hour. Just ask the judge for a recess or some shit like that. Do whatever you gotta do. I'm trying to make sure you're safe, Paris!"

"Okay! Okay! Calm down, Keece. I'll try to call you whenever I can." She rolled her eyes.

Keece grabbed Paris and positioned her on his lap. He kissed her neck, causing her to squirm in delight. One touch from Keece always created a lustful fire inside of Paris.

"Don't be mad at me, baby. I just want to make sure you're safe because if something else happens to you, I'm going on a killing spree." He nibbled on her ear, and Paris closed her eyes, becoming enchanted by his touch.

"Babe, stop that. I'm still sore," Paris purred softly.

"But I'll be gentle."

Paris gave him a look before standing. "Okay. Wait here," she said and walked back into the bedroom.

Keece sat anxiously, scrolling through his phone. He didn't know what Paris had up her sleeve, but he was ready for whatever it was.

Twenty minutes later, Keece heard Paris call his name. He got up and walked inside of the bedroom where he froze on his stride. There were candles strategically placed around the bedroom creating a romantic mood. Paris stood seductively wearing a pink teddy with a matching. Her breasts were spilling out of the cups while the candle light shimmered against her thick thighs. Keece licked his lips, taking in the scene. Paris knew just what to do to make his dick stand at attention.

"What do you think you're doing?" Keece asked, grinning.

"Take off your clothes, and let's get in the shower," she demanded, ignoring his questions.

Keece's eyes followed her body as she walked to the bathroom and removed her lingerie. He quickly followed her, intrigued by the little game she was playing. Paris stood naked by the shower door cupping her breast. Keece instantly took off every article of clothing and walked over to her. He kissed her softly and grabbed her ass. She stepped back with a smile on her face then turned on the water.

"Get in," she told him.

Keece got inside and turned his back toward the water. Paris stepped inside with a bottle of champagne in her hand. Keece gave her a curious look as he took the bottle out of her hand.

"What's this for?" he asked.

"I want you to give me a champagne shower while I suck you off," she said seductively.

Keece's dick stood at attention as soon as he heard that. Paris had turned him on to the max, and he couldn't wait to feel that wet mouth of hers on his dick. She started kissing him hungrily. She then trailed kisses to his neck and down to his ripped abs. When she reached his penis, Paris took her finger and spread his precum around the head. Keece bit his bottom lip in anticipation. Paris then wrapped her juicy lips around his thick dick and started deep throating it as if she was starring in a porno. The sight almost made Keece bust, but he managed to keep his composure.

He poured the champagne as Paris went up and down his shaft. The way the champagne bubbled down her wet breasts made Keece weak in the knees. The hot water was soothing on his back as Paris sucked the life out of his dick. Her glowing skin and wet hair was a sight for sore eyes as she began to pick up the pace. Keece grabbed the back of her head and guided her deeper on his shaft.

"Damn, baby," was all he could muster up.

Paris grabbed his nuts and massaged them gently. She loved giving head to Keece because she enjoyed seeing him so vulnerable. It gave her a sense of power knowing that she could bring the Keece DeMao to his knees. Keece bit down on his lip, trying not to scream out like a little girl. Moments later, he released himself inside of her mouth, and she swallowed every bit. It was the first time she had ever swallowed, and she knew it would drive him crazy.

"Aye, where did that come from?" he asked, still reeling off of his mind-blowing orgasm.

"It came from me." She stood wiping her mouth with the back of her hand.

"Damn, that was that deal. I'm ready to give you the safe combinations and all that," he joked.

Paris smiled and kissed his cheek. They washed their bodies and stepped out of the shower. Paris brushed her teeth and blow dried her hair. After doing her hair and washing her face, Paris walked to the bedroom where she found Keece snoring lightly. She climbed into bed, snuggled closely to him, and drifted off to sleep.

****

"Paris, baby, wake up," Keece said, shaking her.

Paris stirred in her sleep before finally opening one eye. She pulled her phone from under her pillow and checked the time. It was 8:30 in the morning, so she couldn't understand why Keece had woke her up so early.

"Keece, it's too early..." Paris whined, pulling the covers over her head.

Keece yanked the covers back, exposing her naked body.

"Keece, stop playing. I'm tired as fuck," Paris hissed, trying to cover up again.

"Aye, let's go get married," Keece suggested.

"What?"

Although Keece was smiling, he was fearful of rejection. He was afraid that he may have put too much on Paris at once, but he was hopeful. Yes, they were getting back on the right track, but was it enough for Paris to marry him? Keece couldn't control his desire to make her officially his. He had lost her once, and he wouldn't survive if he ever lost her again.

"Marry me."

Paris sat up on her knees. "Are you serious?"

Keece grabbed her hands. "I want you to be my wife. Paris, you belong to me, and if you'll allow me, I promise to be the man that you deserve. No, I won't be perfect, but I'll try my best to make sure that I take care of you and your heart. I know that I've made a lot of mistakes in the past when it came to you, but I swear I'm not on that shit anymore. You'll be my first priority from now on. I love you, baby. I always have and always will." He smiled.

"Keece, I don't know what to say..." Paris spoke softly with tears in her eyes.

"Say you'll take my last name."

Paris looked into his eyes as tears poured from hers. She couldn't believe that he was asking her to marry him. His proposal had made her heart smile. She wanted nothing more than to share her life with him and carry his last name.

"Yes, Keece, I will," Paris said, hugging him tightly.

Keece and Paris shared a sensual kiss for what seemed like hours. At that very moment, Paris knew she belonged in no other arms except Keece's. There would never be another man who would love her the way that he did.

"Come on and get dressed so we can go get married," he said grabbing her hand.

"Like right now?" Paris questioned.

"Yeah. I know a judge who'll hook us up. But we gotta hurry up, unless you've changed your mind."

"No. I'm ready. Come on."

Paris hopped up and went to shower. After showering, she brushed her teeth and began applying her makeup. As she was looked in the mirror, Paris couldn't wipe the smile off of her face even if she tried. She was on cloud nine because she was about to become Mrs. Keece DeMao in a matter of hours. Paris walked out of the bathroom and headed to the closet where she stopped in her tracks. Keece stood there looking so good that she literally couldn't take her eyes off of him. He donned a black button up with a black Armani Exchange blazer. His gray slacks by the same designer were a perfect fit. For his footwear he'd chosen a pair of black Gucci loafers. Keece's diamond earrings shined brightly, and his presidential Rolex completed his entire look. She had never seen Keece dressed up, and it turned Paris on tremendously.

"Girl, hurry up and get dressed before I change my mind," Keece joked, brushing his hair.

Paris sucked her teeth. "Picture that shit," she replied and headed to the closet.

Paris sported her white jumper that was low cut in the front accentuating her full breasts. She slid her feet into a pair of white Giuseppe Cruel Summer sandals. Paris combed down her wrap and parted it down the middle, leaving it bone straight. After putting on her accessories and grabbing her clutch, she walked back to their bedroom.

When Keece saw her, he whistled before licked his lips hungrily. Paris looked beautiful, and he couldn't wait for her to become his wife. He had never been so sure about something in his life. He knew he was making the best decision ever.

Keece walked over to Paris and brushed a strand of hair away from her face. "You gotta be the most beautiful girl in the world."

His compliment caused her to blush. "Thanks, babe."

"I got you a wedding gift." Keece grabbed a box and pulled out a Rolex that was the same style as his. He helped her put it on and adjusted it to fit her wrist.

"This is nice. Thank you, honey," she said then kissed his lips.

"Do you mind if my mom comes along? I told her this morning about us possibly getting married, and she said she wanted to be there. You know she ain't trying to miss any more special events involving my brothers and me."

Paris smiled. "No, I don't mind, I like your mom. But maybe I should call my mom too. I don't want her to be salty at me," she said, grabbing her phone.

"Don't trip. I called her too. It'll be the four of us."

Paris smirked. "So you just knew I would marry you, huh? Arrogant ass," she teased.

"Nah. Real life...I was scared as fuck. I didn't know what you would say, but I'm glad you agreed to marry me." He smiled.

"Of course I was going to marry you," she said, stroking his face.

"A'ight, let's go so we can pick up the rings on the way there."

Keece grabbed her hand, led her to his Bentley, and headed to the courthouse so they could be united as one.

****

Keece and Paris stood face to face as they held hands while standing in front of the judge. Their mothers sat together in the front row as they watched their children become one. Paris' stomach was in knots as she looked deeply into Keece's eyes. She had fought so hard to keep her love for him locked away, but God had a funny way of bringing them back together. An unfortunate situation had brought them back into each other's life, and Paris was so overjoyed.

"Paris Parker, do you take this man as your lawfully wedded husband, to have and to hold, from this day forward, for better, for worse, for richer, for poorer, in sickness and in health, until death do you part?" the judge asked.

Paris smiled. "I do."

The judge then turned to Keece who stood with his signature grin. On the outside, he looked confident, but he was really shitting bricks. He couldn't believe Paris had agreed to marry him. She was the woman of his dreams, and he prayed that God guided him to make the right decisions as her husband.

"Keece DeMao, do you take this woman as your lawfully wedded wife, to have and to hold, from this day forward, for better, for worse, for richer, for poorer, in sickness and in health, until death do you part?"

"I do."

Once Keece said those words, tears began to run down Paris' face. If someone would've told her six months ago that she and Keece would become one, she would've laughed in their face. But the reality was that she was his and he was hers.

"Can I say something?" Keece asked the judge.

"Sure."

Keece cleared his throat. "Paris, I love you unconditionally and without hesitation. That night when we met at the club, I was only interested in *you know what*. But when I got to know you, I realized that you had a beautiful spirit, and I fell in love. I know I've made some mistakes in the past, but I promise to be a better man for you. Today, I give you all of me, and as your husband, I promise to take care of you emotionally, financially and physically.

Paris began to cry harder at Keece's beautiful words. She looked over and saw that their mothers were wiping their tears away as well. It felt good to hear Keece say that she had all of him.

"I love you," she whispered.

The couple then exchanged rings and was finally declared husband and wife. Keece took Paris' face into his hands and gave her a sensual kiss. He stuck his tongue inside of her mouth and gently bit her bottom lip.

"Okay, Keece," Shonda sang.

Paris laughed, breaking their kiss. Her mother always found a way to ruin something.

Keece smiled at Paris and then grabbed her hand.

"Come on. Let's go celebrate."

Paris smiled. "Okay."

After exchanging I do's and promising to love one another for eternity, Keece and Paris, along with their mothers shared an intimate dinner on a yacht that Keece had rented. The yacht rested along Lake Michigan in downtown Milwaukee. The beautiful dark sky was vibrant and the city lights created a multihued effect. Paris couldn't stop staring at her ten karat, rose gold diamond ring. Her previous wedding ring didn't even come close to touching the ring that shined brightly on her finger now.

"I'm so happy you asked me to be a part of y'all's special day. I didn't think I would cry as much as I did," Rochelle said with a laugh.

"Yeah, you cried too much. Your blush was running and shit," Keece teased her.

Paris hit his arm playfully. "Leave her alone, Keece. She's missed a lot of precious moments, so let her bask in this one. And it was *mascara* running, and not no damn blush." She giggled.

He shrugged. "Man, I don't know all that shit y'all females be wearing."

All three women laughed at Keece's silliness while enjoying their stuffed lobster. Their waiter came out and refilled their glasses with more Champagne

"So you weren't around when he was growing up?" Shonda asked Rochelle, unaware of Keece's past family situation.

Rochelle shook her head. "No. Before Keece and I were reunited, I had not seen him since he was maybe two or three years old. Girl, it's a long story that I'll have to share with you later."

"Well, all that matters is that you're here *now*. I can tell that you really missed your sons," Paris said, trying to lighten the mood.

Rochelle gave her a faint smile. "Thank you, Paris. I did miss them terribly."

"Well, can I say how glad I am that you guys finally put your egos aside and got back together?" Shonda cut in. "I've been secretively rooting for you guys for months, and I'm happy that my baby has someone who will take care of her and also protect her. Because Lord knows that last fool didn't," Shonda scoffed thinking about Paris ex-husband, Juan.

"He was a sucka?" Keece asked.

Shonda scoffed. "No. He was a bitch-made punk," she spat, causing Rochelle to choke on her drink.

Rochelle thought her mouth was ridiculous, but Shonda was right on her heels. She was her kinda girl.

Paris smacked her lips. "Ma, he was not that bad," she argued.

"You're crazy! He didn't even know how to change a tire. What kind of shit is that?" Shonda hissed and then took a sip of champagne.

Keece laughed. "Damn, Paris, you was married to a lame. Don't worry. King Keece came to your rescue." Then he kissed her neck.

"Y'all are irritating." Paris laughed.

"So when are guys going to go on your honeymoon?" Rochelle asked.

Keece cut his eyes at Paris. "I wanna go right now, but Paris is trying to go back to work Monday. She's really messing up my plans," he replied.

"Why are you going back to work? You should just work from home since that bastard is still on the loose." Shonda was against Paris going back to work period because she didn't want Chase to find her and possibly go through with his threat.

Paris closed her eyes before responding to her mother. Yes, she was glad that she had people that truly cared about her wellbeing, but at the same time, she didn't want to be a prisoner anymore. Truthfully, Paris wasn't too concerned about Chase because she knew Keece would ensure that she was protected. She felt liberated, and it was time for her to live her life and stop hiding from Chase.

"Ma, I need to get back to work. I'm tired of being in the house. Plus, I'm missing out on a lot of clients and money. Trust me. I'll be good."

"She must be your only child?" Rochelle asked.

Shonda nodded. "Yes, and I don't play about my baby," she replied.

"Don't worry. I'ma have one of my shooters taking her back and forth to work. She'll be protected," Keece assured Shonda.

Paris just smiled at her husband. He had always assured her that she would be protected and taken care for. That's why she knew that she was supposed to be Mrs. DeMao. Keece was Paris' forever and ever.

For the remainder of the evening, they ate, laughed, and talked about future plans well into the night. Paris would remember this day for the rest of her life. Even though she didn't have a wedding, the day was still near and dear to her heart. For her first marriage, she'd had a big lavish wedding. It all unraveled six months later. So Paris couldn't be more satisfied with how special Keece had made the day.

After parting ways with their mothers, Keece and Paris checked into the Pfister Hotel where they became one with their bodies. They made love as if it was their last time ever. Kissing, licking, and moaning were the only sounds that came from their presidential suite. Once their love making session came to a halt, the couple lay in the bed basking in the presence of one another.

As they lay there, Keece finally told Paris what had happened between him and his father. Paris knew Keece missed his father, but he was too proud to admit it. He also told her about his lifestyle and how deep he was in the drug game Unbeknownst to Keece, Camara had already filled her in on the issue with his father, as well as his status in the family business.

"So does my lifestyle bother you?" Keece asked, rubbing her booty.

"Don't you think it's too late to ask that now that I'm your wife?" she joked.

He looked at her. "Nah, because if you had a problem with it, that would've put me in a hard place that I don't want to be in. I want you to be comfortable more than anything."

"Well, I mean it hasn't affected me, so I guess I'm okay with it. But you gotta learn how to come to me when things go wrong. I wanna be included in all aspects of your life. I'm supposed to be your best friend, so when you leave me out of the loop, it hurts my feelings."

"I know, baby, and I promise I'll tell you everything from here on out," he assured her.

"So how much are you really worth?" she asked, changing the subject.

"Fifty dollars."

Paris laughed and smacked his chest. "Stop playing, Keece. How much?"

"Shit, I don't know. Maybe like millions, baby. Probably over twenty mil."

Paris lifted her head and looked at him to see if he was telling the truth or not. "Are you serious?"

"Yeah. I've been working since I was fourteen, and my pops always told us to invest our money, so that's what we all did. Now we're all millionaires, including Big. Plus I don't spend a lot of money."

Paris lay on his chest stunned. "Wow! I didn't know any of this. Your ass has been holding out on me for real." Then she sat up and threw a pillow at him.

"I haven't been holding out. I just don't broadcast my finances. But you know what's mine is yours now. I've put your name on all of my accounts, the house, and even my life insurance policy. I know your independent ass don't need it, but we're married now, so as your husband I have to take care of you."

"Aw, thank you. You just inspired me to stay on my shit."

Paris gave him a juicy kiss, loving the fact that he had finally opened up to her. She could finally say that she had all parts of Keece now.

CHAPTER NINETEEN

"Bitch, how the fuck did you get married when just last week your ass was on a "fuck Keece" tour?" Camara questioned Paris as she held Milan.

She had come to visit Paris on her first day back at work. Just like everyone else, Camara was concerned about her safety. So she decided to bring her lunch and make sure she was okay.

"Girl, I know, It's crazy to even think that I'm Paris DeMao now," she spoke, looking at her wedding ring.

"I'm happy for y'all, though. You guys belong together."

Aimee popped her head inside of Paris' office. "Did I just hear you say that you and Keece got married?" she questioned

"Yes, we did," Paris giggled.

"Oh my God! Congratulations. Okay, I wanna know every detail. Like how did he propose, what did you wear, and where did you guys get married?" Aimee asked quickly and took a seat.

Paris began to tell Camara and Aimee about her special day. She couldn't help but blush as she reflected on her wedding. There was nothing that could steal the pure bliss she was enjoying as a happily married woman.

"Aw, that's so sweet. He finally locked your stubborn ass down," Camara teased, trying to give Paris a high-five, but she didn't return the gesture.

Paris rolled her eyes. "I'm not stubborn. It's called being *smart*. Know the difference."

"Well, you know what that means, right? You're next to jump the broom," Aimee told Camara.

Camara shrugged. "Hopefully...we'll see. I have to make sure that the new and improved Kiyan is here to stay *permanently*. You never know with his crazy ass."

Paris smacked her lips, saying, "Don't do Kiyan like that. He's been good to you for months. Leave my brother-in-law alone."

Camara laughed, teasingly, as she taunted Paris, "A bitch is so happy to call him brother-in-law now. Get your happy ass out of here!"

Before she could respond to Camara, Paris' cell phone rang. She smiled when she realized it was Keece.

"Hey, honey."

"What's up with you? You good?" he asked.

She smiled. "Yes, everything is fine. Camara stopped by to have lunch with me."

"Oh, word? Tell Camara I said what's up. Aye, I called to let you know that I'm going to the strip club tonight with my brothers. You cool with that?"

Paris could tell he had a smile on his face when he asked the question.

"I guess so, as long as you're cool with me going to a strip club with Camara and Aimee." Paris covered her mouth to contain her laughter.

"Paris, you ain't going to no fucking strip club. Why do you want them gay-ass niggas in your face?"

Paris sucked her teeth. "Why do you want them hoes in your face?"

"I'm just going to have a drink," Keece joked.

"Um, you can have a drink at Big's bar. Don't try and play me. You can go, but you better keep your hands to yourself."

"A'ight, baby. I call you later," Keece said before hanging up.

Paris hung up her cell phone as she chuckled to herself. Keece wanted her to be cool with him going to a strip club, but he flew off the handle when Paris mentioned that she might go to one also.

"Keece is trying to go to a strip club?" Camara asked.

Paris positioned the baby on her other leg before answering her. "Girl, yes, but he don't want me to go to one. He's a trip for real."

"So you said it was okay for him to go?" Aimee asked.

Paris shrugged. "Yeah. Why not?"

"Girl, Big's ass better not even try it," Aimee replied. "I don't want no half naked hoes in my man's face."

Camara gave her a high-five, obviously agreeing with her statement. "Girl, I feel you because Kiyan's ass would probably get tempted, and then I would have to show my ass."

Paris shook her head. "Y'all are stupid as hell. Who do you think Keece is going to the strip club with? His *mama*? He's going with y'all niggas." Then Paris laughed.

Camara and Aimee looked at each other before getting up. Aimee raced back to her desk more than likely to call Big. Camara grabbed her cell phone. Paris laughed at their antics because they were really trying to stop their men from going to a strip club.

"Milan, your mama is crazy as hell," Paris cooed to the baby, causing her to smile.

Minutes later Camara hung up the phone and shook her head.

"What did he say?" Paris asked her.

"He told me get off of his line with that bullshit." Camara laughed.

"Since it's my first day back, and I am swamped with work, you gotta go, boo." Paris said, handing her the baby.

Camara rolled her eyes. "Um, I've been kicked out of better places than this. I should make your ass throw up that food you just pigged out on.

"Thanks for lunch, boo." Paris winked.

She walked Camara to the elevator and then hurried back to her office because she had to call the IRS. She knew that would take up most of her afternoon. Paris waved to the security guard who was posted in her office. She was so thankful for the building manager for arranging to have a guard in her space because she did feel safer.

****

Later that night, Keece rode shotgun with Kiyan and Dinero as they made their way to the strip club. When he told his brothers that he'd gotten married, they'd insisted on going out to celebrate. Keece thought that they would clown him, but surprisingly, they showed a lot of support. They all liked Paris and thought that she was the perfect match for him. Keece puffed on his blunt as Bryson Tiller's "Sorry Not Sorry" flowed through the speakers.

"Man, now you gon' have Camara's ass thinking we're about to get married and shit," Kiyan fussed.

Keece scoffed. "Nigga, that ain't got shit to do with me. Stop acting like you don't wanna marry Camara."

"I do, but it'll be when *I* get ready."

"Man, you better lock Camara down before a nigga like me come and snatch her ass up. You want me to be an uncle *and* a step daddy to Milan?" Dinero laughed.

Kiyan slammed on the brakes. "Aye, bitch, stop playing with me before your ass be walking to the club," he threatened, looking at him through the rearview mirror.

"Dinero, you're a disrespectful mothafucka," Keece told him with a laugh.

Kiyan started driving again. "Man, don't gas him up. He just pissed me off," he snapped, trying to hold in his smile.

"Aye, Keece, did you call Pops and tell him you got married?" Dinero asked, changing the subject.

"Nah. I'll probably hit him up tomorrow. I was thinking we should meet up with Pops and squash this shit we got going on between us. I feel bad because he's been trying to reach out to me, but I keep forgetting to hit him back," Keece said, thinking about his father.

"I ain't even mad at him no more. I'm just happy Mama's back in the picture," Dinero revealed.

Keece looked over at Kiyan who was silent. He knew that Kiyan still held a grudge against their father because he hadn't spoken to him in months.

"What do you think, Kiy?" Keece asked.

Kiyan shrugged. "Man, fuck dude. He disappointed me for real. I never thought he would've lied to us for years and then to talk about Mama the way that he did. I held him to a higher standard than that."

"Man, he disappointed all of us, but at the end of the day, he's still our father. And we gotta move on from the shit. One day you might do something to disappoint Milan, and you would want her to forgive you," Keece stated.

"Man, I ain't gon' do shit to hurt my baby, but I'll think about it."

Minutes later, they pulled up to the club and hopped out. Big pulled up around the same time with Case. The five brothers met at the door. When the DeMao clan stepped out, they always turned heads. Women were going out of their way to get their attention. The strippers even took notice of who had walked in and headed straight to their section.

As the brothers made their way to the back of the club, everyone came up to them showing love. Milwaukee was home to all of them, and they were very popular around the Mil. They all sat in the VIP section where bottles arrived immediately. The club was packed to capacity with half naked women showcasing every crevice of their bodies.

Moments later, CP and Rob walked up to their section. Keece stood to greet them with handshakes.

"Congrats, man. I heard your ass signed your life away," CP joked.

Keece chuckled. "Fuck you, but thanks."

"Man, who is this girl you married? Your ass kept her on the low-low for real," Rob stated.

"Yeah, man, you gotta bring her to the shop so niggas can meet her," CP added.

"Y'all will meet her in due time. In the meantime, I'm trying to get fucked up." Keece grabbed a bottle and poured himself a drink.

Big signaled for one of the strippers, who happily sauntered over to him. He whispered something in her ear, and she smiled at Keece. Keece licked his lips as the busty girl made her way to him. She was cute and petite with an ass the size of Amber Rose's.

"Can I show you good time?" she purred in his ear.

Keece nodded and allowed her to position herself between his legs. Future's "Stick Talk" blared through the speakers as she bounced her ass in ways that Keece had never witnessed. He took out a wad of money and began to make it rain all over her, causing her to dance even harder. Dinero sat next to him with a tall thick chick grinding in his lap.

"Oh shit!" Case yelled over the music.

Keece looked up and saw Paris, Camara, and Aimee strolling in. Paris had her eyes fixated on Keece as he quickly removed his hands from the stripper's waist. He couldn't help but get hard at the sight of Paris, who was rocking a white two-piece skirt set. The skirt fit her like a glove, causing her ass to sit up higher than usual. Her hair was styled in wand curls that framed her face, and her painted toes were on display in some Jimmy Choo sandals.

Paris made her way over to Keece and gave him a stern look. "What the fuck? I thought I told you to keep your hands to yourself," she spat and mean mugged the stripper who stood awkwardly.

"Man, I wasn't touching her ass. Come here." Keece pulled her onto his lap, grabbed her face, and tried to kiss her.

Paris turned her face and briefly watched Camara give Kiyan the business. He too had been caught with a stripper in his lap. Big was the only one who had escaped the fire. At the time, he was too busy downing a bottle of Ace of Spade.

"Stop playing with me and give me a kiss," Keece demanded.

Paris reluctantly leaned in and kissed his lips. She still was unhappy about Keece's roaming hands, but she let it go. Keece gestured for the stripper to come over and continue dancing. Paris gave him a look and looked back at the stripper. She was feeling the dance moves that the strippers was performing.

"She gon' have to show me how to do that move," Paris said, standing up and trying to mimic the dance the stripper was doing.

Keece hurried and pulled her back onto his lap, and Paris laughed.

"Paris, don't get your ass whooped in front of all of these people. Why you trying to show these niggas your ass?" Keece asked.

She kissed him. "Babe, calm down. I was just having fun."

"What are you doing here anyway? I thought you were getting some work done."

"I was, but Camara talked me into sneaking up on y'all's asses, and I'm glad I did. You were damn near fingering her. I should get on the main stage and show these niggas how Paris gets down." She laughed, grinding on Keece's lap.

"Go ahead so I can beat your ass."

"Why are you always trying..." Paris stopped talking, and her jaw dropped. Instantly, her heart rate accelerated to a fast pace. Her limbs started shaking. She couldn't believe this person was standing right in front of her, sharing a laugh with Big and Kiyan.

Keece noticed that her demeanor changed and immediately asked, "Babe. what's wrong?" he questioned.

"H-how do you know him?" Paris asked.

Keece followed her eyes and noticed who she was talking about. "Who CP? That's the manager of my shop. Why?"

Paris gasped. "Oh my God! Keece, that's the guy who tried to kidnap me! It's him!"

Keece looked over and saw that CP was looking at Paris as if he'd seen a ghost. Without warning, Keece pushed Paris off of his lap and stormed over to CP. In one swift motion, Keece hit him with a left hook that sent him tumbling to the floor. Keece continued to pummel CP as rage filled his entire body. He was trying to make a statement with CP. He needed him to know that Paris was his and that he would die before he let him hurt her again.

Big and Kiyan tried desperately to pull Keece off of CP. He continued striking his face. All of a sudden, the music in the club stopped and patrons began heading for the door since they were unaware of what was going on. Security came over and pulled Keece off of CP, whose face was beaten to a bloody pulp. Paris didn't know if Chase was dead or alive because he wasn't moving.

"Come on, let's get the fuck outta here before the boys come," Big said, referring to the police.

Camara grabbed Paris' hand and followed after the men as they made a hasty exit out of the club. Since Camara was parked closer to the door, the girls hopped inside of the car. Keece came up to Paris' window. She rolled the window down.

"Aye, Camara, take Paris straight home. Make sure you put the alarm on. I'll be home in a little while," he told Paris.

Paris nodded and watched Keece jog over to Kiyan's car. She couldn't believe she'd just witnessed Keece possibly kill Chase. It felt good to see Chase get his ass whooped for the shit he'd done to her. Even though Paris was satisfied with how Keece had handled him, she couldn't help but worry about the possibility that her husband might catch a murder charge.

"What the fuck, Paris? Why did Keece beat that boy's ass like that?" Camara yelled, weaving in and out of traffic.

"That was *Chase*! He's the one who raped me!" Paris screamed and rubbed her temples.

Aimee gasped. "Oh my God! Are you serious?"

"Damn! That was him? I should've got a hit or kick in my damn self," Camara snapped as she hit the steering wheel.

"I think Keece did enough damage. I hope he didn't kill him, though. I don't wanna see my baby in jail," Paris said worriedly.

"Girl, his ass is still alive. He's just got knocked the fuck out," Camara assured her.

Paris prayed silently that Camara was right. She couldn't bear to be without Keece for killing Chase.

CHAPTER TWENTY

Everyone met up in the parking lot of the construction office. Keece was still pissed and wished that he had put a bullet into CP. During the drive, Kiyan and Dinero questioned him repeatedly on why he had whooped CP, but Keece chose to remain silent until they had made it to the office. They all jumped out of their cars and met halfway.

"Bro, why did you do that to CP?" Big asked again on the spot.

"That's who tried to kidnap Paris. She pointed his ass out at the club. I should've killed that bitch," Keece barked, pacing back and forth.

Kiyan was stunned. "CP? Was she sure?" he asked.

"Hell yeah, she was sure. She started shaking and shit when she saw him. All this fucking time I've been sitting around laughing with that nigga, and he was the one who tried to hurt my bitch." Keece shook his head at the thought.

"So all of this time we've been looking for him, and he's been right in our faces. This shit is crazy," Big said in disbelief.

"That mothafucka was laid out. You think he's dead?" Case asked Keece.

Keece shook his head. "Nah, but he *will be* when I catch him again. This shit got me all fucked up, bro."

"Don't worry about it," Big told him. "We know where he lives, and I know where his mama stays too. He's probably got ghost after he finally woke up. I'm about to go back to the club and get the surveillance tapes before the law does. Meanwhile, you should lay low." Then Big jumped back in his car.

"Yo, I'ma murder his bitch ass whenever I see him," Keece declared.

"Shit, I'm riding with you. We can't let that shit ride, bro," Kiyan agreed.

Dinero chuckled. "Damn, who gon' cut my hair now?" he joked.

Keece shook his head. Dinero had to be the most ignorant person he'd ever known. Leave it to him to make a joke out of something so serious.

"Do it look like I'm in the mood to laugh with your dumb ass? This dude hurt my fucking wife!" Keece snapped.

"My bad, bro, but I couldn't resist that one," Dinero said, smiling with his hands raised in surrender.

Keece grimaced. "Man, come on and drop me off, Kiyan, before I beat Dinero's ass next."

****

"So you just gon' let that bitch-ass nigga hoe you?" Freeze yelled.

A couple of days after the club brawl, Chase found himself at his cousin Freeze's house. Freeze was Chase's cousin on his mother's side. They had grown up together and were practically brothers. Freeze was the person who had introduced Chase into the human trafficking business.

Chase held a bag of frozen broccoli to his swollen eye as he listened to Freeze rant. He couldn't believe that Keece had attacked him in the manner that he did. He understood Keece's rage because he did rape his wife, but he hadn't intended to get his ass whooped that night. It pissed Chase off that he couldn't defend himself since Keece had almost beaten him to a pulp.

After his failed mission with Paris at the bank, Chase went into hiding for several weeks at his mother's house. He even took time off of work. Although Chase had only given her his middle name, he still didn't want to take any chances on being captured by the police. He knew it was a possibility that he was captured on camera at the bank, so he laid low. No one knew about Chase's double life, and it had him nervous that he had almost got caught. So after ensuring that the police didn't have any leads on him, Chase reluctantly got back to doing him. He would go to work and come home most days. It wasn't until recently that Chase had begun going clubbing, and now he was regretting doing that.

Chase had never had any difficulties when it came to selling women, so it scared Chase when Paris actually got away. He knew for a fact that she would go straight to police and file a report. Now, not only did he have to be on guard for the police, he had to deal with Keece and his wrath.

"Look, this nigga got a fucking army behind him!" Chase snapped, not liking the way Freeze was talking to him. "I can't go up against him. Shit, how was I supposed to know that his wife was Paris?"

"Fuck dude and his army! I'm not gon' let him get away with this shit. Nigga, you should be more pissed off than me," Freeze countered.

"You don't think I'm mad as shit? Fuck you talkin' about?" Chase spat, getting more upset.

"You should've sold that bitch, instead of taking her on a fucking field trip where she played your dumb ass. Aye, Tay, who the fuck is this Keece nigga?" Freeze asked his friend.

Tay shrugged, not really wanting to be caught in the middle of the situation. He knew Keece and his brothers, and they had always shown love to him.

"Listen, we gotta hit that nigga where it hurts. Does he keep a safe or something at the shop?" Freeze asked.

Chase shook his head. "Nah, not that I know of," he said, wincing as he adjusted his body.

"What about his bitch? Let's snatch her up again and come up off some money, since her ass made us miss out on twenty stacks."

Chase shook his head at a rapid pace, disagreeing with the plan that Freeze had suggested. "That shit would never work. You don't think she's already protected? Keece ain't no dummy. He probably has all kinds of goons surrounding her. Plus, we don't know where she lives or where she works."

"Didn't you say she was a lawyer? Just Google her ass, and I'm sure you'll find her office. Come on, bro. I know you're not still in love with that broad. Man, fuck her, and let's get this money," Freeze said in a convincing tone.

Chase gave him a dirty look. "I wasn't in fucking love with her! What the fuck are you talking about?"

Freeze twisted his lips, not believing Chase. "Man, you did fall for her. It took you too fucking long to bait her and when you did, she ended up dipping out on you. You almost got knocked because of that bitch. Just admit it. You caught feelings."

Chase waved him off, not liking that Freeze was calling him out. He may have caught feelings for Paris, but he would never admit it to Freeze.

"Look, this nigga beat your mothafucking ass over his wife. He's already shown you that *she* is his weakness, so let's snatch her up and get paid off that shit. Bro, do you know what I can do with that money?" Freeze asked, excitedly.

Chase sat quietly, pondering the thought of coming up off some cash. Since he was now out of a job, he knew the money would come in handy. Something deep down within him told him not to do it, but he was money hungry, and he would do anything to score some cash. He figured he would get the money and skip town.

"A'ight, man, let's do this, but this shit gotta be planned out right."

****

It had been a week since the club fiasco, and Paris was finally getting her nerves under control. She'd constantly asked Keece if everything was okay, and he had assured her that is was. Paris was worried that Keece may have killed Chase, but he informed her that he was still alive. She couldn't help but worry about Chase possibly trying to retaliate and hurt Keece. Of course, Keece had told her not to worry because he knew that Chase was soft. But it was usually the soft guys who shot first.

Paris sat at her vanity applying mascara to her lashes. She had been feeling sick all week and finally regained enough energy to go hang out with Camara and Aimee. She had even left work early because of the nausea and vomiting. Paris had recently tried sushi for the first time and blamed her sickness on that.

After putting on her makeup, she grabbed her purse and was about to leave until her phone rang. It was an unknown number, but something told her to answer anyway.

"Hello?"

"Aye, baby, you still at the crib?" Keece asked.

She looked at the ID screen, "Yeah. Why? Whose number are you calling from?"

"This is Big's phone. Do me a favor, I think I left my cell phone in my car. Go to the garage and grab it for me and bring it the barbershop."

"Keece, how did you forget your phone? You never go anywhere without it," Paris asked as she chuckled.

"I don't know, ma. It's probably because of that good-good you gave me this morning. Got a nigga discombobulated still," he joked.

Paris giggled. "Shut up. I'm walking to the garage now."

Paris made her way to the garage with Keece still on the phone. She opened the door and turned on the light. Immediately, a smile formed on Paris' face as she stared at the brand new black Mercedes G Wagon parked in their garage with a big red bow on top of it. She had always said that it was her dream car, and the sight of it in the garage made her smile from ear to ear.

"Keece!" Paris yelled, running to the car.

"Look inside to see if you see my phone," he said, still playing his game.

Paris opened the doors of the truck and she found two Celine bags in her favorite colors of white and pink. Keece had also bought her two pairs of Giuseppe heels, a diamond tennis bracelet, and a pair of diamond earrings.

"Babe, thank you! This shit is so fly," Paris said happily into the phone.

"You're welcome, baby. I felt like spending some money on you. You like the gifts?" he asked.

"Yes, I love them. Who helped you pick out these shoes? Your mama?" she asked because they were definitely her style.

"Nah, I did it by myself, girl. I know what your ass likes."

"Oh...okay. I was just asking. You really pay attention to me, huh?" she flirted.

"All the time. What time are you going to hang out with Camara and Aimee?"

"I'm going to meet them at Camara's house in a minute. I didn't want to drive by myself," she told him.

Keece released a sigh. "Listen, I told you that you don't have anything to worry about. CP's soft ass is probably hiding because he knows I'm going to murk his ass when I catch him. I'll have one of my lil' homies follow you so you won't be scared. So enjoy yourself and make sure that ass is ready for Daddy's beating tonight."

She smiled. "Okay. I love you."

"I love you too," Keece said and hung up.

Paris smiled and hopped inside of her new ride, loving the way the leather felt on her skin. After playing with the radio and the computer system, she drove off, taking her new car for a spin.

****

Keece sat in his barbershop with Case discussing his plans for his new tattoo shop. Since he couldn't find a building suitable for his vision, he had decided to contract his construction company to build him one. Keece had his crew working overtime just so the building could be ready within the next month or two.

Case seemed eager about entering the tattoo world. At times, Keece wished that Case would've stuck with college and football, but he understood that he was becoming a man. Therefore, he had to make decisions that were best for him. Case already had the artistic ability. Now all he needed was the skills, and Keece knew he would dominate this avenue.

"Have you been going to Ken's shop to watch him while he draws?" Keece asked Case, who was supposed to have been observing one of his associates to learn how to properly tattoo.

"Yeah. He even let me do a small tattoo for this girl. It came out pretty good. I got a picture of it," Case said as he pulled out his phone. He showed Keece the picture, and he nodded his head in approval.

"This looks hot, bro. You should be ready by the time the shop opens up. Just keep practicing because, eventually, I want you to take over and run the shop for me," Keece said, giving him a handshake.

"Thanks, bro. I appreciate that." Case was happy that Keece gave him his stamp of approval. He'd always looked up to Keece and wanted him to be proud of him.

Minutes later, the door swung open, and Riley walked in. Keece hadn't seen her, since his father was in the hospital, which was months ago. She still looked good with her hair styled in her signature bob. Riley looked like she had picked up a few pounds, but it looked well on her.

She walked over to Keece with a smile sketched on her face.

What the fuck does she want? Keece asked himself.

"Hello, Keece. Hey, Case. How are you guys doing?" she asked in a friendly tone.

"We're good. What's up, though? What are you doing here?" Keece asked, skipping the pleasantries.

Riley cleared her throat. "Well, I was in the neighborhood, so I decided to stop in and say hello since you can't answer your phone," she spoke passive aggressively.

"Listen, Riley, I'm not trying to be mean, but how hard is it for you to understand that I don't fuck with you like that no more? Move the fuck on," Keece spat, getting agitated.

He had tried being nice to Riley, but he was clearly over it.

Riley cocked her head to the side, not liking his tone. "How are you going to say that to me like we weren't together for five years? You said that we could at least be cordial to each other," Riley argued.

"Well, shit has changed. My *wife* wouldn't like me being cordial to your ass."

"Your *wife*?" Riley said, stunned by his words.

She instantly looked at his ring finger and noticed his wedding band loaded with black diamonds. Riley could literally feel her heart break as she came to the realization that Keece was officially off the market.

"So, you married that bitch, but I was with your ass for five years and barely got a fucking promise ring! You got me fucked up!" Riley barked, feeling her blood pressure rise.

Keece walked over and stood, towering over Riley. He needed to get his point across to her so she could feel how serious he was.

"Let me set the tone for this conversation. I'm not in the mood for your bullshit, and I swear I'll drop your stupid ass right here, and nobody will feel sorry for you. I don't owe you an explanation. I don't owe you shit. Now take your ass on," Keece snapped and walked away.

"We have unfinished business, Keece!" Riley spat with her arms crossed.

"We don't have shit! Now get the fuck out of my shop."

Riley mean mugged him as he walked away. She turned around reluctantly and left his shop. The tears stung her eyes as she struggled to hold it together. Riley couldn't believe that Keece had actually gotten married. When they were together, they had talked about the day that she would become his wife, but now that another woman had beaten her to the punch, she was hurt and speechless.

Back inside of the shop, Keece became irritated by Riley's little pop-up. He was tired of expressing to her that they would never be a couple again. He didn't know what kind of language he needed to speak for Riley to understand.

"Man, Riley swears you owe her some shit," Case scoffed.

"Right. I'm tired of her miserable ass. Damn! Leave me the fuck alone. The next time she comes at me on that bullshit, I'm gon' smack the fuck out of her."

"Fuck that broad, man. Don't let her ruin your happiness with Paris. It's obvious she's unhappy with herself."

Keece shook his head as he listened to Case's words. There was no way he was going to allow Riley to interfere with his marriage. She would either walk away on her own or she would have to get it the hard way. Either way, Keece was definitely ready for whatever may come.

CHAPTER TWENTY-ONE

Paris sat eating breakfast while talking on the phone with her mother. She had begun to feel sick once again, so she had decided to make an appointment to see her doctor that morning. Keece promised to take her since she wasn't up for driving. Besides, she needed his moral support. Paris stuffed her last spoonful of eggs into her mouth, feeling like it would come back up instantly.

"Ugh, Ma, I've never felt this bad before," Paris complained, pinching the bridge of her nose.

"Oh, baby, it's probably a virus. A couple of ladies at my job were out with the stomach flu. It's a nasty bug going around," Shonda replied.

"Yeah, but mine has been around for like two or three weeks now. I haven't been able to concentrate at work or at home. Poor Keece has been picking up the slack around the house."

Paris smiled, thinking about how helpful Keece had been.

"How's my son-in-law been? You haven't been getting bitchy with him, have you?" Shonda questioned.

Ever since Paris had gotten married to Keece Shonda would make sure that Paris didn't get on his nerves. She thought that Keece was the perfect gentleman.

Paris chuckled. "Ma, why do you constantly ask me that? You do know that Keece works my nerves sometimes, right? He is not the perfect man you think he is."

"I'm just making sure that your spoiled ass don't run him away because you know how you can get."

Before Paris could respond, her other lined beeped. She looked and saw that it was Keece calling.

"Hey, Ma, this is your 'perfect son-in-law.' I gotta go. Love you." Then Paris clicked over.

"Hey, babe, are you on your way?" she greeted him with a question.

"Nah, baby. I gotta take care of something important so my mama is on her way to take you."

Paris sucked her teeth. "Keece, you promised to come with me," she whined.

"I know, but something came up that I gotta take care of. Just call me as soon as you leave and let me know what the doctor said," he replied, feeling bad that he couldn't go with her. He had gotten a tip that there might be a raid on one his trap houses, so he had everybody moving everything out of the spot.

"Okay. Are you going to answer when I call?"

"Yeah, I promise. Look, I gotta go. My mama should be there soon, a'ight?"

"Okay. Be safe. I love you."

"I love you too."

Paris hung the phone up and went to finish dressing.

Minutes later, she heard the doorbell ring. Paris grabbed her phone along with her purse and hurried to open the door. Rochelle stood there looking fresh and fabulous with her jet black hair hanging down her back

"Hi, sweetie, how are you feeling?" she asked giving Paris a warm hug.

"Not good at all."

"Oh, well, come on, so we won't be late for your appointment."

Paris and Rochelle hopped in the car and started driving toward the highway. Paris was quite surprised that Rochelle was bumping Jeezy softly through her speakers. She didn't think a woman her age would like the sounds of trap music.

"So have you started decorating your new house yet?" Paris asked.

"Yes, ma'am. I was going to hire an interior decorator, but I figured I could do the shit myself, hell. Don't nobody know my taste anyway." Rochelle laughed.

Paris giggled. "I know that's right. You're happy about being around your family again?"

"Oh my God! I can't even explain the joy I feel now that I'm able to see my sons whenever I want to. And they've been taking such good care of me. I can honestly say that I'm truly happy now, especially since I can get to watch my sweet grandbaby grow up. I have no complaints at all," Rochelle said on the verge of tears.

She had prayed to have her family back, and now that she did, she never wanted to lose them.

"I'm happy for you. Keece seems much happier since you've come back around."

Rochelle shook her head. "I think that happiness comes from *you*. He really loves you, and I love that about him. I'm so glad he found a nice girl to marry and settle down with," she said sincerely.

"Thank you. I'm happy we finally got over the hiccups in our relationship and can be happy as husband and wife. Even though he dances on my nerves."

"Girl, I know. Shit, all of my sons are a handful."

Paris and Rochelle both laughed.

They arrived at the doctor's office fairly quickly, then walked inside. Paris checked in and sat next to Rochelle who was reading a magazine. After about ten minutes, the nurse called her back, and she was instructed to give a urine sample. After that was done, Paris got her vital signs taken and waited patiently to be examined by her doctor.

"Hello, Mrs. DeMao. How are you feeling?" Dr. Sherwood asked.

"Not good. I've been nauseous for the last three weeks. I also vomited a couple times too."

The doctor looked at the chart before looking at Paris. "Well, I think I may know what's going on."

"What is it?" Paris asked anxiously.

"Your pregnancy test came back positive, sweetie. When was your last period?"

Paris thought for a moment. "It was about a month ago."

"So that explains why you didn't know. Well, we're going to do an ultrasound to see how far along you are. So step up here."

Paris reclined on the exam table, feeling so elated. She had always wanted to be a mother and the thought of being with child made her excited. She knew Keece would be happy as well. Dr. Sherwood spread the cool gel substance across Paris abdominal area and used the probe to take a good look at the baby. Paris smiled when she saw her little peanut floating around inside of womb. She couldn't wait to tell Keece the news.

"It looks like you're about four weeks so far. Everything actually looks good. I'm going to write an order for blood work and a prescription for some prenatal vitamins. Oh, here are some pictures that you can share with your husband. Congratulations again, sweetie."

"Thanks."

Paris cleaned her stomach off and returned to the waiting room. Rochelle looked up awaiting a diagnosis.

"I'm pregnant," Paris whispered to her.

"What? I'm so happy!" Rochelle sang with glee as she danced in her seat.

Paris laughed at Rochelle's little dance move, trying not to pee on herself.

"Okay, okay. I'm back girl. I'm just so excited! You would swear that I was the one pregnant!" Rochelle said with a giggle.

"I am too. I can't wait to tell Keece."

"He's going to be so happy. Come on, let's go eat a meal to celebrate. Hopefully, your ass won't throw it up," Rochelle said, grabbing Paris arm.

Paris smiled at Rochelle, happy that she was excited to be expecting another grandchild. Paris also couldn't wait to share the news with her mother since she'd always said she couldn't wait to become a grandmother. Although Paris was feeling like crap, it didn't rob her of the joy of knowing that she was about to become mother.

****

Keece walked inside of his home a little after midnight. After the long day he'd had, all he wanted to do was eat and curl up next to Paris. She never did call him after her appointment, and he was anxious to know why she had been sick for the last couple of weeks. He walked into his bedroom and found Paris curled up on her side of the bed asleep. He walked over and stood for a minute, admiring the beautiful pout that she wore when she was asleep. Then Keece bent down and kissed Paris' lips, waking her up.

"Wake up. Why you didn't you call me after your appointment?" he asked, caressing her cheek.

She smiled, happy to see his face. "Because I was hanging out with your mama, and then Camara ended up meeting us at the restaurant. Why? Did you miss me?"

He chuckled. "You know I always miss you. Aye, but what did the doctor say?" he asked, hoping that it wasn't anything serious.

"Well, the reason why I've been sick is because we're about to have a baby," she said cheesing from ear to ear.

"For real?" Keece asked with a wide grin on his face. He was so happy that he would soon become a dad.

"Yes! I'm four weeks pregnant. Look, I got some pictures from the ultrasound."

Paris reached into the nightstand drawer and removed the pictures. She gave them to Keece. He looked at them intently, taking in that Paris was pregnant with his baby.

"This is the best news I've got since we got married. Damn, we're really about to have a baby," he said in disbelief, rubbing his hand across her stomach.

"Yep! Are you happy?" she asked, already knowing that answer.

"Hell yeah. I hope you give me a little boy. We need a lil' Keece running around here."

Paris rolled her eyes. "No, we don't need another Keece around here," she protested.

"So when is your due date?"

She smiled. "In March."

"Move over."

Keece climbed into bed with Paris and held her tight. He was so happy that Paris was carrying his first child. He took pride in not having kids all around the city with different women. For hours, they talked about baby names, what their child would look like, and also what kind of parents they wanted to be. Paris was also happy that she would experience being a first-time parent with Keece.

As they fell asleep together, Paris couldn't wipe the smile off of her face if she tried.

CHAPTER TWENTY-TWO

"Man, you whooped his ass bad, Keece," Big said, taking a pull from his blunt.

The whole gang was in Kiyan's front yard sitting around enjoying the summer night. Case and Kiyan were challenging each other to dribbling matches while Dinero was next to Keece seated on the hood of his car. Nights like this reminded Keece of their teenage years, when they would sit in front of the house for hours and just talk shit to each other or meet up with girls.

Keece smiled. "Good. When I catch his ass again, I'ma put a hot one in him."

Dinero shook his head. "I'm still trippin' on the fact that Paris was fucking with him before everything went down. Milwaukee is small as fuck."

"Oh, I knew there was something I had to tell you. I found out who that Shy nigga is," Big informed Keece.

"Who?" Keece and Kiyan asked at the same time.

"Some dude that's locked up. He was Alyssa's boyfriend, and he used to have her set niggas up for him. I heard they were copping plenty of bread."

"See, why would you have your bitch doing that when you can't even protect her? He's all the way in jail trying to set some shit up while his bitch is out here naked. That nigga is an idiot," Keece said with a chuckle.

Dinero laughed. "Well, thanks to him, Alyssa is now fish food."

"You talked to Pops?" Keece asked Kiyan, changing the subject.

Kiyan nodded his head as he bounced the basketball. "Yeah. He called me last week and shit. I heard him out or whatever. I'm not going to hold a grudge no more." Kiyan felt that it was time to finally let the past go so he and his father could move on.

"I'm glad y'all finally spoke to each other," Keece said sincerely.

"So Pops came over to see the baby last week. He tried talking to Mama again, but she wasn't having that shit. She cussed his ass out like he owed her some money. Man, I almost had to pull them apart 'cause she was about to whoop his ass," Kiyan said, laughing hysterically.

Keece shook his head. "I don't know why he keeps trying. Mama don't fuck with him."

They all broke out in laughter because Keece honestly didn't think his father would have the guts to keep trying to apologize to Rochelle. In the midst of them laughing, Camara walked outside holding baby Milan wrapped in a blanket wrapped.

"Why do you have her out here? It's too cold for her," Kiyan complained.

"Nigga, it's like seventy-five degrees," Dinero said, laughing.

"Thank you! Plus she, is covered with a blanket. Anyway, I came out to congratulate Keece," Camara responded, smiling.

"For what?" Kiyan asked.

"He's about to become a daddy. Milan is gonna have a cousin soon," Camara said, kissing the baby on the cheek.

"On what you knocked Paris up?" Big asked, laughing.

Keece smirked. "Yeah, she's like four weeks along."

"Welcome to parenthood, bro." Kiyan said, shaking up with Keece.

"So I'm guessing Dinero's next or Big gon' pop out another one," Case said.

Big frowned. "Shit, you're a motherfucking lie. I ain't trying to get nobody pregnant. I already got the baby mama from hell."

"I wrap up every time, nigga," Dinero added.

Case, Dinero, and Big went back and forth on who would have a baby next. Keece shook his head at them because he knew for a fact that Dinero and Big didn't strap up every time they had sex. After chilling with the crew for another hour, Keece made his way home so he could snuggle up with Paris and rub on her belly.

****

Paris and Keece sat inside of Pappadeaux restaurant looking over the menu. Keece had taken her to Chicago for a little getaway since he had been busy with the construction business. So since Paris had been craving seafood like crazy, he took her to one of the best seafood spots in Chicago.

"What are you going to have?" Paris asked.

"I think I want a steak. I already know what your ass is getting." He chuckled.

"Oh, so you think you know me, huh?" she flirted.

"Hell yeah. I know you better than you know yourself."

Paris rolled her eyes playfully at him. "Oh my goodness. Here you go reaching and shit," she laughed.

"I ain't reaching. I do know you better, and I most definitely know what that pussy do," he said, licking his lips.

Paris couldn't do anything but smile at his dirty talk. She couldn't argue with him on that. He most definitely knew how to please her body. His sex game was the main reason she was knocked up in the first place.

"Yeah, I don't hear you talking now," he taunted her.

"Whatever. If my memory serves me correctly, your ass tapped out last night when I wanted a second round." Paris smiled because she was now the one who was doing the taunting.

Keece sucked his teeth. "Man, I was tired as fuck. I needed a minute to get myself together," he said, laughing.

"Yeah, and a minute turned into you sleeping all night. You ain't shit," she spat, joining him in laughter.

"Aye, but on a serious note, I got something that I'm working on that I can't wait to share with you." He grinned.

"Like what? What is it?"

"It's a surprise, but I know you're going to like it."

"Keece, come on and stop playing. I need to know," she whined.

Before Keece could respond, his cell phone rang. Since he didn't recognize the number, he decided to hit the ignore button. After ordering his and Paris' food, his phone rang again from the same number. Keece wanted to ignore the call again, but he thought that maybe one of his brothers may have been in trouble.

"Hello?"

"Can I speak to Keece?" a male voice asked.

"Who is this?" he asked, ready to go off.

"I have some information that you may want to hear regarding your wife, Paris."

****

Two days later...

Chase and Freeze sat outside in the parking lot in front of Paris' job. They had finally agreed on a plan that would get them the payday that they needed. They would snatch Paris as she exited the building and take her to Freeze's house. After getting her situated, they would then call Keece and demand a sum of one hundred thousand dollars. Of course, he would arrive to deliver the money. Afterward, they would drop Paris off at a park unharmed. Even though they had gone over the plan a million times, Chase was extremely nervous.

"You sure this is where she works?" Freeze asked impatiently.

"Yeah, nigga. I see her car over there. Be patient."

Freeze huffed becoming more impatient. "Damn, what time does the bitch get off? It's going on seven o'clock."

"She posted on her Facebook page that she would be working late today. Listen, if she'll be the only one in the office, it'll work out better for us because it won't be any witnesses."

"If that's the case, go inside and lure the bitch out here. Then we can just grab her and hit it. Shit, I'm hungrier than a mothafucka," Freeze complained.

Chase thought for a moment about what he could say to Paris to get her outside. He knew that she would be terrified once he showed his face. He was still a little apprehensive about kidnapping her because he knew the consequences could be deadly. So he decided to persuade Freeze to go instead.

"I think it would be better if you go in. She'll probably have a heart attack if she sees my face."

Freeze nodded. "A'ight, I'll go in and snatch her ass, but watch my back. If you see anything suspicious, call me, nigga," Freeze warned him, getting out of the car.

Freeze pulled his hood over his head and walked briskly into the building. Since Paris had switched offices, they'd had to rely a lot on Google and do some heavy digging to locate her new office.

Freeze pushed the elevator button and waited nervously for the doors to open. He stepped inside and pressed the button for the seventh floor. His anxiety had spiked to an all-time high, causing his body to shake.

Finally, the elevator alerted him that he was at his desired floor. The doors slid open. As soon as he stepped out, he saw a man step in front of him swiftly and hit him with a metal object. Freeze felt so much force from that hit that he knew his facial bones had broken. He fell to the floor trying to steady his body, but it was too heavy. After struggling for a moment. He finally blacked out.

Chase sat in the car as he anxiously shook his foot. Freeze had been inside of the building longer than expected, and Chase was on the edge. He grabbed his cell and began to text Freeze. Without notice, the car door was snatched open and Chase was pulled out of the passenger seat.

"What the fuck!" Chase yelled as he fell to the ground.

He looked up and saw two men with ski masks covering their faces. His heart rate began to accelerate as the two assailants looked down at him. Chase tried to get up, but was kicked in his face. Suddenly, Chase became dazed as his head fell back on the pavement. The man lifted his foot once more, where he came down hard on Chase's face again, knocking him out.

****

Chase awoke from a deep slumber, trying to recollect what had transpired before. All he could remember was getting snatched out of the car and being knocked out. As he opened his eyes, he saw Keece sitting on a table going through his phone. When he looked to his left, he saw Kiyan, Big, and Dinero standing and talking to each other. Immediately, Chase began to panic and squirm in his seat, but he soon realized that he was tied up.

Keece noticed his struggle and started laughing.

"You ain't getting out of here, playboy," Keece said, teasing Chase.

Chase knew deep in his heart that it was the end for him. There was no way that Keece would let him walk out of here alive when he had already raped his wife and had just tried to kidnap her. He said a silent prayer, asking for a quick death so he wouldn't have to suffer.

Keece approached him slowly. "So you really thought you were gon' get away with kidnapping my wife? Nigga, are you that stupid? Did you really think it would be that easy?" he barked, feeling his blood pressure rising.

"I wasn't the one trying to kidnap her. It was my cousin. I only wanted to apologize to her," Chase lied, hoping it would get him out of the predicament he was in.

"Bullshit. Your boy, Tay, called and filled me in on the entire plan. I left Chicago so fast after he called me. You and your hoe-ass cousin thought y'all were about to come up off my money."

Chase cried. "Man, it wasn't even like that."

Keece raised the baseball bat that he was holding and swung it at Chase's left knee. The sound of bones crushing filled the warehouse. Chase yelled out in pain, feeling like his entire leg was on fire. Keece then swung the bat at his right knee, producing the same result.

"I told you that nigga was a bitch. Yelling and shit like a little hoe," Big joked, ready to put a hot one in Chase.

"Come on, bro. Spare me this one time," Chase cried, feeling as those his legs had been severed from his body.

Everybody in the room laughed as if Chase were a comedian on stage for the first time. Keece was a little upset with himself because he couldn't believe Chase was bitch-made, and he didn't even know about it.

"Bitch, he ain't your bro, and fuck you. You wasn't thinking about that shit when you were about to sell Paris to the highest bidder," Kiyan spat.

Dinero walked next to Keece who was glaring at Chase. "So, how much you be getting from the human trafficking shit? Is it worth your life, my nigga?"

"You know what, CP, or whatever the fuck your name is? I can't believe you thought that dumb-ass plan of yours was going to work. As soon as I got that call, I started putting my plan into motion. Since you thought you were going to take Paris from her job, I made her post on her Facebook page that she would be working late. You see, I knew your stalking ass was following her on her social media sites. That's why I made her do it. Then I had somebody go park her old car in the parking lot, so you could think she was really at work. After that, I had some of my little homies waiting in the office and parking lot for your stupid ass. Oh, yeah, your cousin is a done one. He went swimming in Lake Michigan," Keece said, smirking.

Chase cried harder at the fact that his cousin was dead. There was no telling what kind of death he'd experienced, and he couldn't help but feel terrible.

"Man, just shoot me!" Chase yelled out.

Keece sucked his teeth. "Nigga, you don't call the shots around this bitch. Aye, Case, lower the rope for me."

Case turned on a switch, and a rope was lowered down to where Chase was seated. Keece walked over and wrapped the rope around his neck, tying it tightly. Chase tried to resist, but found it impossible to. Keece then walked back in front of Chase, lit his blunt, and blew smoke in his face.

"You fucked with the wrong mothafucka when you hurt my wife. Do you know what kind of emotional damage you did to her? Thankfully, she's strong and managed to move past the shit every day. But you're a sick bitch. I can't believe I used to allow you to run my business and cut my hair. I hate it had to come to this... Nah, I'm lying. I'm about to enjoy this shit." Keece took out his phone and snapped a picture of Chase.

"I just wanna make sure Paris sees how you spent your last moments. Case hit the switch," Keece instructed.

Moments later, the rope began to retract back toward the ceiling, carrying Chase. The rope that was around his neck began to squeeze tightly, cutting off his air and circulation. Chase began shaking viciously as he felt his life being sucked away.

Minutes later, he urinated on himself as his airway became constricted. Keece looked intently as Chase struggled to breathe. Seeing him hanging in the air from the rope created a satisfactory feeling. He now had one less problem on his hands.

"That was a creative way to murk a nigga, Keece," Dinero said, giving him props.

"Hell yeah...except him pissing on himself. Stanky-ass boy..." Big joked.

Keece turned to them. "I wanna thank y'all for always having my back. Even when I was locked up, y'all held shit down for me with no questions asked. Just know whenever y'all need me, I'm here to ride with y'all," Keece said sincerely.

Kiyan laughed. "This nigga getting all mushy on us and shit."

"I'm serious, nigga. I appreciate y'all having my back."

"You know we got you, fool," Big said giving him a handshake.

"Now that this shit is out of the way, let's go to George Webb's. I'm hungry as fuck," Dinero announced.

CHAPTER TWENTY-THREE

Three months later

Keece sent Paris a confirmation text letting her know that he would meet her at the doctor's office. He was excited because Paris was getting an ultrasound done and this would be the first time that Keece would see the baby. He was grateful that Paris' pregnancy was going great, except for Paris' occasional mood swings and morning sickness.

Since Keece was low on gas, he pulled up to the first gas station he saw. He hopped out and used his credit card to purchase the gas.

Moments later, he pulled the pump out and began to fill his tank up. Out of the corner of his eye, he noticed a woman with a young kid. At first glance, Keece saw the familiarity in her face and then he realized that it was Riley's mother.

"Hey, Ms. Carrie," Keece spoke, waving.

The woman stopped in her tracks and looked to see who had called her name. When she realized it was Keece, she gave him a faint smile and walked over to him. Keece looked down at the little girl and smiled. She was such a cute baby. Keece wondered briefly how his child would look.

"Hey, Keece, how have you been? I've been meaning to call you," she said, giving him a friendly hug.

"Oh yeah? About what?" Keece wondered why she of all people would be trying to reach out to him.

"To see what's going on with you and Riley," she answered.

"Ain't nothing going on between us. She and I don't speak," he spat, twisting his face.

"Well, don't you think y'all should?" she quipped.

"Um...no...I got a wife and a baby on the way. I'm not trying to deal with Riley like that."

"So you don't know?" she quizzed.

"Know what?"

"You and Riley have a daughter."

to be continued...

Text the keyword "Jessica" to 25727 to receive a text message when Keece and Paris 3 is released!

ABOUT THE AUTHOR: Charae Lewis was born and raised in Milwaukee, Wisconsin. Reading has always been one of her favorite hobbies, and she was eventually inspired by other authors to write her own story - ultimately challenging herself to write a book. Charae loves writing because it simply takes her to another world where she can design the rules. She also writes for the benefit of young people going through the same types of situations that she pens. Ready to take the literary industry by storm, Charae is currently working on her next novel, and one day she aims to grace the NY Times Best Seller List.

Please feel free to reach out to me on my social media sites:
FaceBook: Charae Lewis
Instagram: Charae_Rozay
Twitter: Charae_Lewis